More praise for Evan S. Connell's *The Alchymist's Journal*

"Evan Connell's book raises a memorial to prodigious dreams. . . . We may at times feel as though we have stepped into a new place. We may get an inkling of what the world felt like some centuries before it assumed its modern contours."

—Sven Birkerts, *The New York Times Book Review*

"A beguiling work, Joycean in its outpouring of words, sometimes as mad as Paracelsus himself seems to have been . . . It is, in many ways, a crazy-house mirror of our own irrational times."

—Richard Marius, *Boston Review*

"A new work by Evan Connell is always a cause for celebration. . . . *The Alchymist's Journal* is a daring fictional feat perfectly mixing style and substance. . . . The true alchemical master here is Connell himself, writing in full form and powers."

—Don Skiles, *San Francisco Chronicle Review*

"A feast of words, a poem, a tract, a set of pseudo-documents . . . This is as much a cautionary tale about the dangers of the imagination as it is a celebration of its powers."

—*The New Yorker*

"A densely contrived, meticulously researched meditation on the historical moment . . . *Alchemy's* concepts—part mysticism, part rough science—exert a fundamental appeal that Connell has polished with the storyteller's art and the historian's grasp of detail."

—Albert Mobilio, *New York Newsday*

"Connell achieves great beauty in luxuriant prose that seems to have sprung from the late Middle Ages. . . . *The Alchymist's Journal* commands thoughtful attention, its surface resplendent with forgotten lore of alchemy, science and love."

—*Publishers Weekly*

"By choosing a language that names the experience of the unconscious through an alchemic vocabulary, Connell is able to create an almost fantastic landscape reminiscent of Hieronymous Bosch."
—Alberto Manguel, *The Washington Post*

"Connell reintroduces us to a world view in which matter and spirit, mankind and nature, scholarship and worship, are one."
—*Los Angeles Times*

"Connell's trademark style—the probing curiosity, the deliciously, intensely poetic language—is ideally matched to the exoticism of medieval science and mysticism, with their elusive elixirs and metaphysical passions."
—Sarah Cahill, *The Village Voice*

"*The Alchymist's Journal* probably should be read at least twice. . . . It is the sort of uncompromising endeavor that deserves to be read with the care and consideration that obviously went into the writing."
—Frank Wilson, *The Philadelphia Inquirer*

"*The Alchymist's Journal* is a striking tour de force. . . . Evan S. Connell has long been one of the best American novelists."
—*Newark Sunday Star-Ledger*

PENGUIN BOOKS

THE ALCHYMIST'S JOURNAL

Evan S. Connell, the best-selling author of *Mrs. Bridge* and *Son of the Morning Star*, received an award in literature from the American Academy and Institute of Arts and Letters in 1987; in 1988 he was inducted as a member of the Academy. He lives in Santa Fe, New Mexico. *The Alchymist's Journal* is his fifteenth book.

The Alchymist's Journal

Evan S. Connell

PENGUIN BOOKS

PENGUIN BOOKS

Published by the Penguin Group

Viking Penguin, a division of Penguin Books USA Inc.,

375 Hudson Street, New York, New York 10014, U.S.A.

Penguin Books Ltd, 27 Wrights Lane,

London W8 5TZ, England

Penguin Books Australia Ltd, Ringwood,

Victoria, Australia

Penguin Books Canada Ltd, 10 Alcorn Avenue, Suite 300,

Toronto, Ontario, Canada M4V 3B2

Penguin Books (N.Z.) Ltd, 182–190 Wairau Road,

Auckland 10, New Zealand

Penguin Books Ltd, Registered Offices:

Harmondsworth, Middlesex, England

First published in the United States of America by

North Point Press 1991

Published in Penguin Books 1992

10   9   8   7   6   5   4   3   2   1

THE LIBRARY OF CONGRESS HAS CATALOGUED THE HARDCOVER AS FOLLOWS:

Connell, Evan S., 1924–

The alchymist's journal/Evan S. Connell

p.   cm.

ISBN 0–86547-464-8 (hc.)

ISBN 0 14 01.6932 6 (pbk.)

1. Paracelsus, 1493–1541 — Fiction.

2. Alchemy — History — Fiction.

I. Title.

PS3553.05A79   1991

813'.54 — dc20   90–28844

Printed in the United States of America

To William D. Turnbull

*Heaven has become empty space for us,
a fair memory of things that were.
But our heart glows, and secret unrest
gnaws at the root of our being.*

JUNG

The
Alchymist's
Journal

FROM my father I learned astrology and medicine. Aged sixteen I entered the university at Basel but went away dissatisfied. I traveled to Würzburg yet there again I could not find what I wanted, nor at the metallurgic school of Sigismund Fugger. In the Savon valley at the convent of St. Andrew dutifully I listened to august bishops—to Mathias Schacht of Freisingen, Mathias Scheydt of Rottgach, and to Eberhardt Baumgartner. Yet all for what? I have traveled to Munich, Regensburg, Noerdlingen, Amberg, Hongary, Meran, Krain, Maehren, St. Gall and Kaernthen, encountering emptiness everywhere. Out of Germany I wandered through Italy and France to the gloomy Netherlands, to England, Scandinavia and Russia, but what did I gain? Aged twenty-three I returned to Basel, there to be crowned Professor! Hah! Like some mud-plastered Swiss boar reeking dung I pretended to wallow among obsequious compliments while plucking feathers from the tails of malt-worm pseudologues in blue velvet that strutted, preened and croaked from the dais like pigeons on a ledge. Now look at my reward! Say that I clutched a plough, greased wheels, served cabbage or played the lute—all would understand my trade. I would be welcome in any province. But for challenging dead doctrine and seeking the universal catholicon I am reviled by medicasters lost at the back of the world rammy and wet, blaring like goats to prank up themselves—gowned vultures, cock-chafers jumbling on the bed, temple thieves boasting more toes than teeth, maskers with legs aspew like arches under a bridge and tails more noteworthy than their heads. Oily saltimbanks! Brangling knaves! Fabulists! Strokers and scrapers with the eyes of blood-letting Saldanian chymists that prescribe a dying man twenty poisons for one. Mewling advocates of Greek sophistry. Red-brindled Hungarian pigs that mistake the Danube for the sea. What confounds them they curse as Beelzebub's work! Curs barking after genius that think to bite my shoe! Hah! What are their names in the street? Sycophants vomiting yellowed lies, sons of cuckolds that grope toward paradise in a milk-maid's crotch. Indentured almond-pickers prescribing slough water and sow-piss, brewing emetics of rinsings. I hear better medicine whistle from a cheese-monger's bung. So they cry out how I inveigh upon Doctors, Councillors, Chirugeons, green-pizzle Pantologists. And this is true. But why? Because I know what they are made of because Nature has put her autograph on them. I despise the house which is faulty and lets in rain. Jiggish imposters! Rogues jabbering dead prayers! And there are others so numerous I do not name them. I have met plenty.

I AM called Heretic for asserting truth, called Luther's Ass—impious—since I look to causes instead of gaping with disbelief like inhabitants of asylums that misjudge reality. I was not born Geber's cook—my mouth a passport, ormolu my fortune. Neither was I ordained to be a fiddler nor iniquitous privy-rat. I am no silver-sucking roach or pocky Quean. Neither would I be strangled by any woman's garter. So how would I accept the argument of lesser men with brains as blank as slates that ratify what others dictate? I hear the east wind blow through their souls. Scabby lechers on rattly shanks, atheists, flea-sprung wits, sons of potters, whoremasters scraped out of sheep, fleering grinning moldy mountebanks, liverish prostitutes hawking greasy nostrums with fingers that twitch and jerk to see a bulging leather purse, servile boasting quacks in shit-stained breeches, malsters, sodomites fornicating upon rear stoops with spaniels or kitchen help—how many mumble and glory at the title of Physician? Doctor Slop! Puppets skipping on a showman's wire with brains delivered to them backward like a clyster, drips from a waning moon, thoughts scattered like nails in a peddler's pack, emptying wormy cups while attending Egyptian athanors, hop-whistling rancid quarreling puking disciples, meat-shop philosophers ignorant of true medicine's requisite—Sapientia! Tetrick bloat-herrings waxed fat with deceit that set up practice among hedgerows from Prague to Geneva and market vermifuge less salubrious than frog guts in a wine glass, all spouting windy proverbs for love of a florin! Summer breeds not half so many mosquitoes as those accursed horse pintles ripped with lice! The severity of their offences I will transcribe on their foreheads because I know their balance-sheet.

THEY say I am full of knots. This is true. Like a bear cub was I suckled among pine forests. Like damp moss do I cling to what I knew best early in the morning. How could I wear gossamer? Why would I go prancing through female apartments? What man is sweetly turned if in the province of his birth they do not weave or spin silk? And I was born Theophrastus! I am the Prince of Physicians—monarcha medicorum. Aureolus I am called and so be it. Was a tongue endowed with speech? No. It is the presiding spirit grown impatient with vacuity since every creature is compacted of elements. Therefore I condemn all those that distil by prescription as Chymists. Are they like a good tailor that carefully cuts a cloak? No. I denounce them because they would lay straw in a sick man's bellie. Juggling sophists! Catchpoles! They do not encounter infirmity but at the declining. Gravely do they march forth like judges to give peremptory sentences of death, thereby expecting to be honored as prophets with deep prescience! Bah! Unctuous rakes honing after wonders that neigh toward other men's wives, shanks wet with rot, stout on porridge and mutton and stinking like a goblin's fart. Back-sliders with the elevation and ostent of serpents that would subtract honor from jackals by their presence. So they come pouring across good reports, and does not a pig call a pig gorgeous? See the consul of Astorza! Niger! See Muffel parade through Nuremberg! Hah! But this is not their end. This is not all. I know of others. Black bougiers with kneecaps made of horn which if they quit praying would bite their tongues for devotion, slip-weary toothless maskers with raddled bones struggling hard as January to hoist one foot across the door-sill and scratch their balls. Croups to affright Asmodeus, drizzling yellow or green as a rainbow. They collect like August flies at the lip of a milk-pail to drink and discuss philosophy. I have watched them draw out figures and hawk wax talismans or amulets filched from a grimoire at Ratisbon. Philtres with grainy powders they provide, hence they denigrate with covin the true art of alchymy. Has not all jurisdiction its limit? They would plunder what cannot be replaced. Yet as the guilty by their rhetoric exercise unwarranted dominion, so the moon indifferently presides above good and evil. This is loathsome! How are the travesties of invidious art expunged? Groveling kabbalists know less than children shut inside a narrow room who because they have observed little must doubt the wealth of exteriorities. False doctors like vile preachers go lying and masquerading and mincing across a stage spun out of hope, flea-stung tumorous carcasses indentured to worms mistaking turds for topaz. How do they know the neck of the afflicted? I alone am monarcha medicorum that through unremitting study has become Prince of Physicians and therefore they hate me. Such is the lot or malison of genius. I bid them warm their buttocks in Satan's vestibule! I do not copy inferiors. I am Paracelsus.

CACOPHRASTUS! So they snap their teeth, declaiming vituperative poetry composed in hell for my benefit. Cacophrastus! Yellow cringing curs snarl and bark. The least hairs of my breech display more learning than their mightiest. My shoe-buckles shine brighter than Avicenna and Galen in conference. Theophrastus am I!—skillful, zealous, adept at the Holy Kabbala, arch-enemy to distemperature, advocate of theology, ascetic defender of freedom, illustrious pharmacist, bald foe of folly. Am I not Theophrastus Bombast von Hohenheim? I am Helvetius Eremita, Philippus, Suevas, Arpinus, Germanus. Or I am the Luther of physicians—Lutherus medicorum. But what difference does it make? I heal patients abandoned by charlatans to sickness or death, restore youth to the aged with marvelous elixirs. And by our Lord I would this gleaming pate might fend off gnats as well as I fend off academic sophistry. Hah! What good is a shining coat-of-mail and buckler? Why gag on stinking panaceas falsely concocted by apothecaries in sculleries? Dizzards! Graziers! Chymists swarming through filthy basements! Vermin begot to brew up foul broth! Dung-prophets! Quack-salvers! None can equal Paracelsus. I am wiser by seventy than all such cod-merchants. Thisselwarps! Whifflers! Daubers! Puffers that coagulate, sublimate and distil—tending bubbling apparatus toward what? I would sooner tabulate every butterfly in Holland. I am the most puissant and numinous doctor on earth, ruled not by the motionless fabric of constellations but incessant study. There be a more pregnant sense to my doctrine than their wits construe.

𝕴 HOLD all secrets of nature, Magnalia Artium, by which God endows a great physician. Let windly raving clotpoles claim I am drunk. I am lucid. If I knew not all bones and varieties of human flesh and where each was placed, how could I choose the

palliative that each wound needs? Leech-doctors say I am ir-
reverent—coarse and uncivil—because on Saint John's Day I
sprinkled with gunpowder and sulfur the fatuitous books of by-
gone theoreticians so they went up in smoke to vast applause
from students, which is what ancient science merits! Rheumy
academics join hands to clap against me. Why? Because I il-
luminate the fount, progress and fall of their tedious conceit.
They parade in sheep's russet, parched brains riveled like apples. I lift my hind leg at them! Costermongers! University catechism is a mildewed cloak for pedagogues hatched in a viper
pit wistly dreaming antique fable. Why expound the opinions
of others—Dioscorides, Galen, Macar? What is learned by
rote? No reliance have I set on Avicenna's consorts because
Nature is the physician, not I. It is she that composes, not I.
From her alone I take my orders and study the art of her pharmacies—behind what leaf she writes each virtue, in which box
each is kept. Not in Mesue nor Lumine nor Praeposito. No
teacher have I met surmounting this world save God, snakes,
magic and angels. I say there will be dowsers and spagyri and
Archei and they will have Quintum Esse and tincture, then
where will your soup-kitchens go? What will become of quacks
that give up a patient to die while working out his complexion
from stools and piss? Joskins! Drovers fixed at their poison!
Wicked, wrong, unjustifiable—so do they brabble against my
meteorics, my physics, my theories, my practice. How might I
seem less than erroneous or strange? What greatness is there
that was not first maledicted?

PSEUDO-PHYSICIANS suppose that by jugglery and cunning they can cheat Nature out of her dues, thereby acting with impunity against the manifesto of God—behavior at once intolerable and specious, a summit of vanity. And for the novelty of constructing artificial systems why disparage familiar treatment? Nor should a doctor pluck apart a sick man's wallet while prevaricating, ramping—spewing foaming gibberish at spotted invalids weak with anguish who conclude this must hold meaning—because such art does not consist of healing the sick but of creeping toward favor with the rich and powerful like some moldy itinerant smiling and bowing, scraping muddy boots on the step of a nobleman's kitchen. Well, it is natural that there should be crafty swindlers laying hollow claim to the honored title of alchymist while scheming after coins, darkening the moon, sifting down like famished locusts whistling depravity, glossing deceit, doubtful of what they themselves have uncovered. How ingeniously they contrive to answer urgent questions posed by desperate innocents—praising agate liquefied, jaspar metamorphosed, frost congealed, or the marvelous values of excrescence. Bah! I hear them spout inanities while stuffing contributions into their split breeches. Who has not seen it?

THE truthful physician prescribes nothing without its merit, disdaining immedical calamities, avoiding what is mendacious or absonant. Neither will he lie, cog or foist restoratives extracted from leper skat and maggots on credulous patients. I see the moribund that fall subject to phlegm or deliracy sacrifice a fortune to apothecaries puffed up with turgent titles—

sails plumped on empty wind—purveyors of fraud greasing their fundament for love of a Swiss franc. Weasels flaunting velvet caps! Dogs trot forth to sniff their vomit! Chickens clustered in a knot provide more nobility, peacocks choked with rage sound less vain and stupid. As if gabbling fraud might rinse their slimy mouths! As if the Holy Ghost of Christian theology should countenance imposture! Lacking skill enough to carve initials on a cherrypit, Cuman asses capering about in lion-skins, ulcerated flatulent druggists with oat-cake faces, three-fingered magicians quick to mulct apoplectic curates— they traffic lotion to soothe the spirit while Lazarus lies howling outside the gate. Christ bid them greet the arrow at mid-flight or collapse in joint depravity with the inward grace of donkeys whose latter vent winks open more modestly than their hearts. Grazing sheep would give up grazing to see such Turkish medicasters. What brains they own they keep sealed in bottles beyond the moon.

𝕴 HAVE heard doctors aspire to the wisdom of forest apes while espousing an imbalance among humors: phlegm, bile, blood yellowed or black. Rot! Disease hides externalities that are its cause, selecting the most susceptible organs for degenerative goals. Men fall subject to more illnesses than a horse and computation by planets is but one aspect. I say sickness arouses waves of heat throughout the body because its constituents have been twisted, tied into knots. Consequently, balance is restored with assuasives such as essentiam antimonii, aurum-potabile, oleum solis or materiam perlarum, arcana quintae-essentiae, aquavitae and so forth. And I believe man cannot enough praise God or give thanks with all diligence for his generosity in providing these because they suffice. And one morning I think all of this will be heard as clearly as the cataract of the Rhine.

Now what injures a man is what heals him, therefore similars are good. Does the liver seek its medicament in sugar, manna, honey, or a polypody fern? No. Like affects like. Shall heat be a cure for cold or the opposite? Seldom in anatomy's order. It would be wild disproportion to find a cure in contraries. If a child should ask his father for bread would he be given a snake? Hence they are not physicians that prescribe acid if alkali is needed. Gall must have what it asks, the liver and the heart as well. Why? Because nature admires logic.

There are several kinds of salt in man that devour and gnaw like hidden fires and one may kindle the next. This is true also of wolves and other animals whose bodies are surfeited by such salts as arsenic which crawl about among the organs putrefying and digesting. Now, just as we are taught through the seething of these minerals how food is torn by interior viscera, so we make further discoveries with the preparation of alum or the fuming of lime. Things are sought and found, yes, but sometimes prove difficult to separate.

The carpenter thinks out a cottage—how it should be built—and then he goes to work. Not so the physician who does not think out how a disease should be, since he did not make it. Nature invents disease and therefore knows its constitution, so if a doctor would know what to do he must acquaint himself with what she has to teach. The carpenter may hew down a tree and work with this as he needs or pleases. Not so the doctor, because medicine does not wish to be altered—like the garden of Attalus where nothing grew except venomous plants.

MALADIES that afflict mankind are not inherent but arise out of sources directed against the cycle which penetrate and suck and dilute our vital essence. I say that Magnes Microcosmi since it is composed of urine, blood, excrement and hair— when it is applied to the corpus it will absorb vitality like a sponge drawing water, thereby alleviating the inflammation of harmonious members due to congestion by precipitant fluids. But illness acquired from a patient manifests itself elsewhere because all things correspond, hence the toxicant released from a body must contaminate others. Remedies invert, breeding their own abuse.

BECAUSE the earth has been enclosed within a vaporous sphere as the egg is enclosed within a shell and cosmic influences converge toward a nucleus, it follows that epidemics develop when miasma pollutes this involucrum—which is not strange. Possibilities could not be limited by our knowledge of them since who among us pretends to fathom God?

SOME argue how man collects understanding from his own self and from constellations, so that if one's star is favorable one may learn everything. But if each man was born to inherit the kingdom of God how shall he be a child of constellations which are doomed to perish? And therefore how should one seek wisdom except where it resides beyond the stars and planets? Who could believe that there lives concealed inside an egg the animus of a bird with all of its members and feathers and whatever else pertains thereto? Similarly who would say of gold that within it lies a recipe for universal healing? Yet just as the white and the yolk conspire to bring forth a ringdove or a finch, so must time, nature and alchymic art conspire to fertilize the Grand Catholicon. This is because of nature's predictability since everything that takes place must coincide with reason.

WHAT is heavier than gold? What weighs less than the wind? What could be whiter than a swan yet blacker than a crow? What is more hurtful than a serpent? Are not these things all in Nitre? Yes. Professors cry out with a single voice, saying fix the volatile and volatilize that which is fixed, then you will find the universal panacea. But a sensual eye deprived of light— what does it perceive except darkness? Thyme is seen to bloom throughout the year while the crocus has a moment in autumn. Experience does not run one way but many thousand ways.

I SAY the martiality of a sickness is enhanced by its aura blossoming from the center yet clinging to its locus. Thus, if a magnet shall be placed upon the center it must attract a widening aura, thereby circumscribing the flow of disease. But how so? Because metallic particles infest man's blood. By contrast, the scent of an orchid travels from its petals into the atmosphere and this aura cannot be circumscribed. I do not know why. The curve of thinking has no end.

I SAY it is clear how incorporeal pernicious influences are capable of burning and devouring, such as vitiation of the surrounding air which secretly encourages impure vapors seeking entrance to the body, or the convulsions engendered by drinking decadent water so that a victim falls down writhing and vomiting. Thus the pharmacology of heaven should be studied much as we diagram the veins of a suffering patient if we would devise an efficacious cure for astralic impairment because analeptics subside under the reign of malevolent planets. Illness withers if the regent compounding it does also and is a mandate from God which we should recognize, since he administers to our necessity. If we scorn a light above, how does it reveal our path? How does it assist our progress?

I HAVE said that chymists who seek out nature's probities or inclinations should consult within themselves, only then addressing externalities. Why is this? Because all things proceed from pole to pole, as we learn from Egyptian tombs where painted noblemen march forward to the past, preceding their descendants in hieratic order. Now this is harmonious, marvelous and immutable.

I HAVE said that alchymists plot the course of each disease with its premonitory symptoms because a disease is a plant that will develop into a tree if it has not been rooted out while it is young. I say a child is able to cut down an oak soon after it springs from the acorn, but given time enough this will require a strong man with an ax. And I say further that men must see by what operation nature conducts her work in order to revise the meaning of what they think.

Pseudo-alchymists that labor against quicksilver, sea salt and sulfur dream of hermetic gold through transformation, yet they fail to grasp the natural course of development since what they employ are literal readings of receipts. Accordingly they bring baskets of gilded pebbles to sell, or drops of vinegar in cloudy alembics—futile panaceas meant for a charnel house. This is false magistery.

Thousands proclaim themselves Adept that have dealt little with spagyric matter. By such conceit they disenfranchise the conscientious aspirant. Puffers abound—monk-bellied wizards proposing deleterious recipes in lieu of knowledge. Granted a crock of paste I doubt any could fix a fractured pot. Their persuasions are wretched, false and degenerate, their devices precarious.

I have watched charlatans with the help of greasy advocates cloaked in malfeasance skipping and bleating merry as goats. But as a metallic stone attracts and repels iron particles according to its animus, so does every man attract or repel effluvia for evil or good. And what he is, that will he be at his death since the spirit does not deviate from itself. Consequently each man endows the atmosphere with a vestige and register of his life. And I say that as the angry light of dawn will diminish a candle, so does alchymic magistery eclipse and shame the artifice of squint-eyed gut-bucket butchers serving slabs of deceit. I would not award them Christian burial. I would hang them upright like Diogenes to scare off crows. Cucurbit, alembic, furnace, retort—only thus shall we hear the human predicament annunciated, since within our Philosophic Egg begins a fabulous process of fermentation, distillation and extraction.

CACOPHRASTUS! Hah! Cacophrastus is how they deride me because I endorse principles, not catechism. Mock-doctors swaggering round about in spangled coats! Foals that presume themselves stallions! Buggers leading one another so that if one tumbles in a ditch the others follow, unable to separate their brains from their asses. Piebald knaves! I have watched them coaxing victuals out of monks, I have seen the ravens that supervise murder rise screaming from their perch, for leaven and ferment are Christ, and I say Verbum Domini is the word of the father that has become Matter and is the material food of the soul. And such a word is present in each object in which it dwells. And I have seen them worse than Archbishops order up relics to fumble at a sick man's mouth. But I say sickness is neither endogenous nor constitutional, and a mineral seed is required to engender what once was sown into the earth by our Lord God at a time when he regretted the creation of man.

I SAY that whatsoever fills up a man's heart shall overflow into his mouth. And what his heart desires, that do his eyes seek after. And things irrevocably incline toward similitude because they have some rational or active virtue that directs and counsels them—as fire experiences the urge toward fire, water toward water—which accounts for the passionate flight of the soul and the body's deep unrest. Now I say all of this will be understood by those with a legacy of interior senses while to others it must seem incomprehensible.

I SAY the heart is an instrument of very great magnitude whose greatness cannot be expressed. The mind as well—this is very great and nothing can emerge from its sphere that was not drawn in. And whatever the heart has attracted or whatever was drawn into the mind I say will expend itself searching for an exit. And it is perilous to live ignorant of this relationship.

I SAY that six Tempers dominate the mind, whereby they govern and rule over humanity. These are passion, fright, alarm, joy, envy and desire. Therefore the imagination must be supervised since no place is too far for it to go and each mind impresses another, wherever it reaches. This is because not one being is able to survive apart from the next, nor from the Almighty, because all divide His wisdom.

EACH being possesses a Chaos, yet if transported elsewhere it will die. If that Chaos be subtle, its being is gross, or if gross, we find subtlety within. Therefore a corpus should be gross if it would glide unharmed through aether, much as gnomes with subtle bodies can proceed through rock. Even so, rigid matter is capable of piercing supple matter just as a stick is thrust into water or a stone may descend into the depths of a pool. Conversely, whenever the matrix does not take offense it is possible to extract a substance, which is the case when fishes are withdrawn while leaving the river unperturbed. So does base mineral hope to improve or glorify or transform its status. And that this may occur cannot be doubted. The omnipotence of God flows unrestricted.

WHAT vast surfeit of disclosures men catalogue upon deficient understanding! To assess an object below or above the animus presiding at its birth or to prize some creature more or less highly than its creator must injudiciously subvert both values, which is how we behold existences doubled by the looking-glass. Therefore we should estimate qualities not by their outwardness but by what they deposit within.

BECAUSE every item is equivalent in goodness to the next, as the carbuncle is not better nor worse than tuff stone, nor evergreen than cypress, so each time we valuate gold above silver we do this out of greed. Both are excellent. Consequently our judgment is developed not through wisdom but through lamentable logic. Now, should a dog fall sick it will devour grass, but would this be suitable treatment for sick men? No. Yet how very often I remark similitudes, and I think egregious pharmacopeia astonishes me less than the gratitude of moribund patients. How is this? Possibly by virtue of imagination we are able to find what we seek, a faculty derived from above since it is evident how stars preoccupy themselves with men.

𝕴𝕿 IS true that stars habitually sympathize with mankind, but which mercies proceed from the mansions of planets? A physician after he calculates his patient's horoscope may deduce an origin to malignancy and prophesy its end. However, each disease boasts five causes—each subject to five aspects—thus no interpretation should be thought infallible. And it is true that proficiencies contribute to failure, so emptiness comes riding. Obstinate doctors adhere to foolish diagnoses more tenaciously than starfish clinging to a barren shelf, but as I am a prudent physician I do not gape upon antique charts drawn for musty lectures. My flesh, my blood and my bones constitute the merchandise I have given up for knowledge. And my spirit have I offered as pawn. And I believe God encourages me to know, but also to doubt.

𝖂HY would a man be anxious to eat and drink and breathe? Because he is conjoined with elements of food, water and atmosphere. Or why does he avoid the cold? Because without warmth he would shiver miserably and complain. This is true because we are made of mutual associations since we have been coupled to all and do not live apart from rudimentary influences, just as we have criminals that flourish and profit beneath planetary conjunctions. Therefore I say the alchymist must understand cosmology because a doctor that treats only the effect of disease is like one that would excoriate and drive winter aside by brushing a little snow from his door.

I SAY the body demands familiar nutriment for support, albeit we need not chew bones to replenish our bones nor swallow and digest veins to regenerate our veins. The living corpus manages to subsidize each necessity, although it is hard to explain how this is accomplished. By what method does bread transmute itself into blood? Nevertheless this occurs, and upon great similarities of hermetic art we anticipate a transmutation of dross, which implies universal regeneration.

TERRESTRIAL and sidereal worlds converge upon mankind so that if any pharmacist would mitigate or alleviate fatal consequences, such as edemata from French plague, he must learn what is implicit. Hence an understanding of herbs is good and it is wise to appreciate Laudanum which is very strong. Now, cinnabar commonly is florid but with albification it can be instructed to simulate Lead, by whose virtue it expects to acquire importance. Thus, every animate substance or creature would modify its attributes while latencies must be sought. Even so, a sapient chymist will memorize the accustomed station and rising of stars if he seeks to maintain tendencies within a pattern of their setting.

MAN's reality is but an exposition of forces and essences identical to congeries on a higher scale which represent the firmament. And beside and within us all is reflected until we ap-

nd ourselves as well as the circumstances of our environment. Thus we attempt to perceive, foresee and augurate. Did
not William of Paris at his laboratory construct a Brazen Head
which nodded, beckoned and spoke to visitors in the voice of a
man? Accordingly we manifest more than brief conjunctions
drawn of flesh, bone and nerve. Upon measurable degrees we
exemplify the cognizant universe. Therefore we must not be
fictive but represent a palpable quintessence, which was the
ambition of our Creator.

IF WE wish to illustrate the several properties of mankind
would we not trace in miniature a precise copy or replica of our
cosmos? If so, then what persuades us to reiterate and duplicate mistakes through treacherous dissimulation? Is it not
more logical to collaborate toward a melioration of Lead,
thereby to form and guarantee what we anticipate? By day we
are wont to clasp hands and replenish our lives with honor while
by night we turn obligations into cobwebs, deceiving ourselves
under nets, entanglement and falsehood. What beggary is
this? Have we not ourselves become beggars begging at our
own door?

OFTEN have I talked with Oporinus of a path to the Citadel
where an inimitable Infant slumbers, encircled by dragons. I
have told Oporinus that lineage and privilege mean little, that
only distress has meaning, since which of us is exempt? And I
have explained how if an alchymist's heart play false so must his
prescription. Sooty empiricks puffing and blowing make wrong
turnings. Divided ashes lie estranged.

𝕴 HAVE taught Oporinus how nothing concerning us be declared irrelevant and foreign. Why has God endowed men with
thought unless they should apprehend their predicament? For
too many is thought considered a vacant entity, but this is mis-
guidance. Thoughts have ponderable crystalline shapes inex-
plicably formed of nutritious components within the soul much
as ice crystals develop in freezing water. Hence, we may impose
upon all men our disposition toward maleficence or beneficence, generosity or selfishness, since thoughts being formed
of quiet volition may be thrown like icicles into the mental
spheres of others. Why? Because the world's huge frame is
known to encompass all and the focus of meditation appears
very great.

𝕴 HAVE advised Oporinus to scrutinize ancient manuscripts
because each opens against its opposite. I say he that observes,
studies, and learns during his tenure on earth shall be dressed
with gold during the Resurrection, while not one that has loitered should aspire to superiority. This is because exploration
leads upward.

𝕺PORINUS would have our secret delivered into his hands. I
respond by asking how he would catalogue the structure of
rainbows, or if he be employed with Nilotic darkness, or if he
has found absolution. Let him think privately on the melioration of nature and reflect how it is impossible to grasp what is
first or last, or take hold of the first that is not also last. So do we
annotate the circularity of Man and we call this ubiquitous

since it is identified with its subject, and no man has discovered how to escape. Should Oporinus climb as high as heaven it would be there.

I HAVE said that in God's presence the most execrable vices of our world disseminate. How is this explained? I point out how treasure flows to chattermag niggard hucksters marketing pinchbeck remedies meant for a Lazaret while the best endure calumny, ridicule, neglect, ingratitude—but to what purpose? Look at what has occurred since the beginning.

LET us assume the throne of heaven was framed within and that every corporeal benefit has been tabulated. Say that a physician controverts himself at midnight, then he could be no itinerant hunched on the door-step of humanity. Neither is he pseudo-medicus or imposter quick to interpret the allegoric journey of a pilgrim, having met in each some hollow glory.

MANY will charge according to their expedient how upheavals and the deaths of kings are adumbrated by comets approaching, yet our worldly lot rests on the palm of an Indecipherable who is its commencement and its end, who displaces sceptres and crowns and tumbles down the mightiest. So must the worst and finest tumble in dust upon august authority, commingled with a universe of streaming shadows.

DOMINANT planets and various stars spread their glory between Flanders and Brazil. Others thoughtfully conceal their light, for what emprize we do not know. Similarly, invidious spirits often deceive or hide their employments from the inquisitive novice. Yet between microcosm and macrocosm every item stands related, albeit we hear much opposed logic formed in concert with strange denial.

I SAY the impetus of ascending planets invigorates animals with harmonious organs no less than minerals or vegetables. We ask why. But what is planetary exhalation save its vital elixir? We see one patient get up and walk away from his bed while for no cause his neighbor vomits and writhes and dies, so it is impossible to contest the power of heavenly light. We are no more devised from insensate clay than is an herb blossoming out of mud.

SHOULD it be God's will to instruct an alchymist at his art He will dispense understanding at the appropriate season. But if by this wisdom He concludes that any man was unfit or should He decide that irrevocable mischief would ensue, then that sanction is withheld. Neither would God undertake to show one man for a principality so that others crowd up against him piteously bleating—or go trotting behind him like sheep after a ram. And he that fails to read blackness at the beginning shall fail at his magistery.

I HAVE said men descry what pleases them because what appears reasonable, that is what they approve. Out of Electrum Magicum they make mirrors which are fundamentally conjoined, as Jupiter conjoins with Venus, since this is nature's scheme and geniture. Hidden causes. Future portents.

$\mathcal{T}$HE beneficial aspects of numerous herbs have been concealed, as are their insalubrities, yet we know how to discover them just as we are able to perceive the dispositions of cattle which never have learned how to speak or explain themselves. Why is this? Because nothing moves on the somnolent seadeep nor in the firmament that was ordained to thwart us, neither fish nor plant nor animal nor bird. All matter is subordinate to the enduring and imperial quest of humanity—its premise. Was not man appointed to explore? Was he not royally baptized? It has become his mission to dazzle the elements. How swiftly he strides forth dressed with jewels to confront the universe. One that wrought miracles they called Galen—Paradoxopoeus—which is the essence of every man. And I say that prodigies which exceed their measure draw destruction on their wake.

$\mathcal{N}$ow, some find great virtue in the herb Centaurea, yclept Isiphilon by Chaldees, which if powdered and intermingled with lamp-oil and the lapwing's blood and set to burning—all those clustered around will cry how they are witches, and say of one whose face lifts toward heaven that his foot yet touches earth. But in so doing they make up a vitious black tincture which provokes almighty God. Groping, tense, men split their brains. They seek to use the wind.

$\mathcal{I}$ HAVE said that things proceed less by lottery than election and humanity's passage appears wrathful, senseless, aberrant, replete with desperate biting, while the stipulations of life are complex illusions resembling colors in an artist's picture, being not in fact yellow or blue or green, merely seeming thus to the eye of the beholder.

I BELIEVE illness substitutes for the spectrum of health its own hue—monarchical and threatening. Pliny the Elder has counted up three hundred varieties or sorts of disease but I account others, curious disaffections to every part. And I say that those afflicting us differ from those past, hence new distillations must be ordered. All objects and phenomena have their hour.

As THE sky possesses constellations so is each man mightily constellated within himself. Then why is he unlike animals or plants or metals that do not deviate from what they are? Why is he alone cursed with a necessity for transmutation? What is incommensurable about him? What urges him to emulate the grison, the fox, the goat, the blood-drinking nightswift? I say that if he would reclaim the nature of his inheritance he must be born again. And I say miracles of the soul exceed heavenly dispensation.

I BELIEVE providence contemplates the blind mole squirming through abysmal darkness and declares its vision adequate. Why? Because to look further would encumber this poor thing with unremitting discontent by exposing the tenebrous walls and limits of its existence. So do we observe timorous men who, perceiving that they have burrowed up toward daylight, hastily dig themselves downward into comfortable obscurity. Still others like foolish birds standing on a withered bough chatter with amazement at the dawn. Others lift both hands to praise the incipient day as night slips west. Providence apportions to each—to each man, beast, insect and mineral—the animus of its being.

Now, if earth be a cryptogram burning with significance— the House of Man in which ubiquitous houseflies predicate brief lives—let us equate the Holy Spirit to a glow-worm. Does not the humblest caterpillar symbolize transfiguration? Therefore let us say quick-silver represents man's conscience whose existence must be verified, having lapsed into desuetude. We see mercuric particles cling to the rim of a dusty crucible, hence we are entitled to say of our conscience that it endures, that it refuses to forget.

Minerals sink, feathers float, serpents upon their course change direction. We do not know why. Quick-silver escapes from alluvial gold—aureate sperm of cinnabar. Why is this? Meanwhile fumbling neophytes submit to misjudgment by Macar, by Galen, by Dioscorides. Even so, they anticipate success! But I say alchymic magistery cannot be conferred by diploma nor through philosophic reflection, nor by those souffleurs that burn charcoal, since being duped on their own ignorance they make dupes of others. I avow that as God spoke radiance was formed, departing from its limb. Then God spoke further, confused elements became separated and what was chaos understood its balance.

Rain falls to the earth not all at once but drop after drop because if it is poured down too abundantly it would destroy everything, just as if a gardener should inundate his plants. From this it is evident how nature distributes her benefits. Therefore the soil of any province tends toward infertility through exhaustion and lies unconscious for long intervals. Similarly, those remote mines which provide silver and gold often exhaust their energy and insist upon millennia of rest before they consent to additional labor. Now this is because minerals germinate and grow like wheat from their elementary matrix, hence it must be useless to contemplate or cry aloud for valuables that do not exist.

When at the end of time all things throw aside their cover every chymist and physician must stand up to be recognized so that we learn which kept to the foundations of science, which did not. Then all that were conceived and flourished emptily and stood notorious behind clap-trap recitals greasily prevaricating—I say their gullets will enlarge at the hour of their disgrace! What do they teach about Pliny's herbs? Have they learned the three parts of wisdom? And how was it that those promising vast wealth to others are themselves importunate beggars? Cacochymists whose tongues ride before their wits like a gentleman's usher! Alleging familiarity with Avicenna of Bokhara, with Velascus and with De Vigo—how do they call themselves learned? Times return, rhetoric yields its measure highest to lowest, logic makes a circuit. Hah! We will count how many rich and redoubtable physicians tucked flagrant ignorance beneath chit-chat to the detriment of reliable doctors.

I say those that truthfully prescribed will be distinguished from muck-hill daubers and guild-hall apprentices. Each deserves his merit, so each shall acquire the palm. Proscription to such swaggering glistering rogues that exult with the title of Alchymist but oppugn the Art, boasting how they know anatomy that cannot identify tartar stuck to their own teeth. Liars! Fugitives! Horse-leech fops! Executioners! Purse-milkers! Yet as the tare is plucked out of ripening wheat so must the melody of pretence reverberate until Whitsunday. The murderer does not escape the crushing wheel, the thief a gallows-loop, the fish its appointed net, the fox his destined hunter.

Because we have made illustrious promises let us keep them albeit the earth quiver underfoot, since to be perceptibly swallowed and wholly to disappear is less dishonorable than egregious dissimulation. There is but one single instrument laboring mightily toward perfection, which is grace within the soul. Lies corrode a susceptible heart and the universe resembles a Harp or a Lute since every occurrence resonates elsewhere, as the son is known by his father.

Be diligent, I have told Oporinus, because the mind proves adroit at generating monsters, since as we draw shapes upon canvas or wood and reconstruct our similitudes with marble so does the mind formulate basilisks which act against us— contriving aspects and molds of grim apprehension. But why? Because nature acts out of habit, she considers only one way suitable and from this she departs with reluctance to create aberrations. Why is this? We could as well ask what accounts for the soft and feline influence of the moon.

I WOULD have Oporinus learn how undines beneath the surface long for sunshine and how their magnetism contrives to pass through impregnable rock for the pleasure of gnomes. Nor should this be disputed, since we know all things aspire to consanguinity. All experience summer and have their winter, all know the taste of fruit.

I SAY we are kept from seeing aetherea by the fallibility of our senses and therefore the mind's eye opens to assist these inadequate organs. Now this is most true with herbs or plants because they teach better lessons than stultified pedagogues pawing and braying from the rostrums of colleges. So have I taught Oporinus about this herb called Matuchiol yclept Heliotropium, which revolves according to the sun. If collected beneath the sign of Leo and wrapped in fescue or laurel and accompanied by the sharpened tooth of a wolf, then no man shall hear a single word uttered against him, only peaceable words. And if he fall asleep on this herb then he could not lose his property to a thief. Moreover, if this herb should be secreted in a chapel where women go that have slighted their vows with copulation—well, they cannot walk past. Or a woman that has clasped Urtica to her breast—she would not succumb to deleterious fancy. Also, there is an herb called Celandine which is gathered where swallows nest, or eagles, that if any man accept it together with a badger's heart he will beat back enemies, annihilating them in argument. Furthermore this same herb if it be laid against a sick man's brow——if he should die he would rise up singing with a great voice. Or the leaf of Periwinkle if eaten together by any man with his wife, they will lie down in love. This much is true and natural. But of the Mandrake which is alleged to groan or shriek when it is torn out of the earth, I am not persuaded. I do not claim to have heard this voice, albeit I listen for cries of anguish. I am positive that God has given to these herbs inexplicable virtues and powers which free men from infirmities to the end that they might sojourn a little longer. And I am convinced of how death itself cannot imagine the fatal circumstance, but strives eagerly and diligently in order that it may not overlook the appointed minute, proving obedient to its master.

I HAVE said that all metals labor with disease, except gold which enjoys perfect health by the grace of elixir vitae. I have taught Oporinus how this metal is sweet and exhibits such goodly luster that multitudes would look toward gold instead of the generous sun overhead. In fixity or permanence this substance cannot be exceeded and therefore it must gleam incorruptibly, being derived from an imperial correspondence of primary constituents which makes it capable of magnifying every subject, of vivifying lepers, of augmenting the heart. Conceived by our gracious Lord, it is a powerful medicament. False gold, which is a simulacrum boasting no remedial virtue, assaults internal organs and therefore it should be abjured, since the alchymic physician repudiates meretricious matter.

We must not keep true gold beyond its measure but distribute what we hold, allegorically reminding each man of an earthly choice he is obligated to make between damnation and bliss.

OPORINUS longs to know the components of imperative minerals. So do many dig deep yet glance by the royal vein, mistakenly posting their elevation against some shadow cast at daybreak. I have explained how seven metals coalesce in a private hour, which is the mystery of electrum and a source of corrective medallions, of sigils and bells to benefit the impropriator. Now, if a paralytic wears a ring pressed from this metal he will rise up and stagger away without assistance. Epileptics or spastics will recoup their faculties. Others also profit, because this substance defies corrupt or antipathetic regents while radiating and condensing the influence of host planets. That is why electrum was utilized by the Magi and Chaldeans. But I would teach Oporinus how men undo themselves in the egg which hatched them. So are they brought to assize.

I HAVE warned my famulus to note how stars on their progress confer blessings. Still, like the mind they subject humanity to various deceits and provide less guidance than surpassing folly. Therefore, with sidereal phenomena infinite patience may be required to identify and solicit one unwavering light among fickle multitudes. And such is the legacy I would leave which I admonish him to respect, since whatever a man thinks or accomplishes, or what he teaches or what he hopes to learn, must have its right proportion. I say it must follow its line and hold within the circle to the end that nothing may exceed its circle, so that there be no crooked thing and the balance be preserved. Water rushes downhill full of desire to unite with the ocean. Heaven exhausts itself, new times come.

𝔑ow I am grown old. It is useless to swim against a current, I will turn and go home. I will go to the place I know best—Einsiedeln—to the episcopal see on the tumultuous Salzach, and I will live in the corner house. I will return to the Hermitage where in the water sliding beneath my window I will see reflected the stones of Hohensalzburg fortress. It is time.

𝔑ever have I known Thy peace, Lord. I have not been touched. All of my life was I a pilgrim, a stranger. I was a stranger, alien, a pilgrim. So let there be sung the first and seventh and thirtieth psalms, and let a penny be given to a poor man by the door with each singing. Such is my will and testament who was christened to honor the Greek from Eresus— Tyrtamos. And I have descended from the soldier that was Conrad Bombast, feudal tenant to a count of Wirtemberg, and my father Wilhelm, who was no community bath-chirugeon but an illustrious doctor that got his licentiate at Tübingen. Aureolus am I nominated by feckless disciples licking my heels hoping to flatter me. And my members have been carved out by God with my conditions and properties and habits bequeathed from that in-breathing of life where things are awarded to men. I do not fear death. Has not the serpent Ourobouros sacrificed himself to himself for the birth of knowledge? Does not wisdom born of adversity dispel subsequent affliction? So much do

I understand without understanding, who was christened Theophrastus von Hohenheim, because I would not argue the proceedings of God.

ARRIVED this day out of emptiness some scrofulous itinerant with his remedy for universal mischief. Serious in aspect, pocked like one half-dead of plague, looped about his neck a green silk ribbon with three octangular medals displaying a new moon and the sun beneath an unfamiliar constellation whose relevance I could not guess. His clear pitiless eyes did not blink—consummate proof of a rogue without goodness to his being, on whose tongue the Lord's Prayer would fester like monkshood. Should a man's soul be scourged he may quote celestial spirits and make diagnoses, but as he shall depart from rectitude so must he be absent from paradise. Therefore my visitant was no physician.

Rumors of a wandering magus . . .

I REMEMBER that he cast no shadow when he shuffled toward us fragrant as a dead mouse or a sulfur pit, rich in shabby rags grilled by the sun——one hand trembling, rachitic, putrescent, colorless eyes plucked out of yesterday's corpse. Children whistled, dancing behind his back. Women held their skirts. Men stood bewildered and unquiet, worried over ambiguities contrary to reason in the pour of the light. If our gracious Lord be omniscient how should this contradiction be devised?

BY SOME private impenetrable sign he signaled to a familiar in the marketplace, so I reflect upon the ways men recognize and notify their equals. Do we frame ourselves at will?

I WATCHED him at twilight scribble the name of a spectre with a seal in the hour of Mars which he gave to a crow and muttering over this bird he commanded it to be gone, whence followed from that region where it flew dreadful thunderclaps, evil clouds and rain and reddish phantoms in bursts of splendor, as though he brought a plurality of worlds.

THEY say his journey began when he fled his father's house at the age of twelve like a butterfly tethered to a string, racked and furious—secreted inside the pommel of his sword that conducive white powder Laudanum—a child eunuch crowned with ivy and foxglove, surging irresistibly toward the ages. He was not engendered like other mortals, I think, nor would have it so. How else does one explain repetitive misfortune?

I HAVE heard that by mystic intercourse with Jews, shepherds, barbers, Romanies, hangamen, acrobats, herbalists, geomants and minnesingers he drew forth knowledge. And each met quick welcome since not one but had a singular message to impart. Consort of rogues, peasants, tapsters, wheelwrights, thieves, jugglers and sectarians, at ease with the devout or impious, vulgar or learned, like some clumsy windy peevish drafthorse he drank, stamped, and belched along the highroad to reproach all that stood amazed. And the preservation of a tortured body some believe he confided to his mind.

OPORINUS has told me how he avoided women, that he disdained venery, but I hear he found good reason since he was gelded at a secluded place where three ways meet by an unknown hag while he was a youth. Thus he grew up impotent, emasculated. In his work he fulminated against women—cursing, spewing venomous hate—until at last overwhelmed with disappointment he returned to the village of his birth. There he scribbled and raged and denounced the world. In his forty-seventh year on a chimney corner bench of the White Horse Inn at Salzburg some swift complaint or miasma befell him and without a word he died, having three days previous dictated to the notary Hans Kalbsohr his last testament which I think was duly heard by five Salzburg men and one Steffan Waginger of Reichenthal, and the servant Clauss. His precious implements, palliatives and medical texts he bequeathed to a Salzburg doctor, Andree Wendl. Twelve guldens in coin he left to his executors, Georg Teyssenperger and Michael Setznagel. And to the six witnesses another twelve guldens each. It was the day of Saint Rupert's festival when he died, which in that year fell upon Saturday. He chose to be laid where the poor are buried.

THAT he is gone seems unnatural. Here was one that had urged gold out of idle brass, brought forth rejuvenating essences, and at his pleasure undertook commerce with witches, afreets and dwarfs while traveling from town to town on a white horse saddled by Beelzebub. Could such a magician disappear? Perhaps all things that we consign to loss are transmuted, otherwise they must vanish into nonentity. Then where should we search for remnants of generation? No doubt all complete their turn, yet I think that upon each dissolution we mark a new ascendant, a new beginning.

I SUPPOSE all perishable things revert to their origin while the sentiments that had excited them perish also—possibly excluding the heart. I have been told of thieves who assaulted the master after a banquet, and robbed him and threw him over a cliff, which brought about his death. Yet others have said he drank a cup of powdered diamond. In any case I look for him to return since the integrity of his being corresponds to the unity of the world.

𝕴 AM told he wrote many books, although just five or six authentic manuscripts gray with mildew have been recovered from queer places—attics, cupboards, scuttles, hollow walls. Habent sua fata libelli. The unbounded torrent of his thought I could not appreciate. Concerning his sword, which disciple inherited such a rusty weapon? No matter. As in chiaroscuro where is the light without shadow?

𝕳 E ASSERTED that alchymy was founded at that quadrivium where astronomy, philosophy, and ethics conjoin with our Noble Art—which prevails since it is suffused by sympathetic reflection. But if so, why do we persevere at enormities? Misapprehending the world, do we seize a broken ladder ascending from hell to a sanctuary overhead? If man is but halfway from an abyss why should he choose obstructions?

𝕾 AY the Magisterium has been explored, what remains occluded must be the nature of its progress—which cannot be described for upon it lies the seal of omnipotence prohibiting mankind from mighty acquisitions that harbor the lodestone of misuse. Bejeweled queens, sceptered regents, aged couples copulating, hermaphrodites, venomous serpents, fiery hoops, dismembered dragons, galloping horsemen, flowers, rams,

wedding, divorce, calendars and citadels, regenerate salaman-
ders, human corpses—thus have I heard the master testify to
what was best or least within the fructifying vocabulary of symbol. Beset by angelic dreams, I think he was born to subdivide
and cast the horoscope of our intransigent world.

𝔑ot until the solution has been met with adequate proportion shall matters disclose themselves to the novitiate, he said.
Hence, no man is entitled to complain that bitter misfortune
has thrust him apart nor look to a bright wheel rising. No, we
reimburse ourselves. Luck walks a crooked line, granted. Still,
very much of what I hear I subject to long probation.

𝔗hings have been left unfinished for their purpose, nothing
can be complete, he said, stroking his bald head. Trees sprout
individually, yet do not make boards alone, neither does clay left
to itself become a finished pot, nor is mankind different. Say we
look up to the firmament for guidance, what is there to apprehend our necessity? Toward the reaches of insensate chaos we
exert ourselves without hope. Our lot is not three but one. So
he spoke, and by such logic does evil intertwine with good.

𝔑ow say you were elevated to Knighthood, he proposed, of
what value would be gilded spurs or a golden bridle? Of what
use is authority that punishes and castigates—satisfied within
itself to boast and revel or to feast and blow shining trumpets?
Because heaven's provenance was, is, and forever must be the
heart, why should God look down to applaud vain pageants?

WHAT is humanity, he asked, if not some barbarous exhibit? Dependent upon jewels, prototypes of miscreation desperate for accomplishment, avid, desirous, half-gowned in purple, offering philosophies cheaper than seaweed, what are we but painted walls agreeable to see which crumble rottenly within? Galled, fortuitous, mummers swallowing rhubarb and turbith, haled in pieces by envy, driven down headfirst to perdition and riveled, mice that selfishly snatch up another's bread, do we not rake the earth to banquet on our cousin's anguish? Glozing titles, are we more than apostles of useless discord with thundering bowels? So he discoursed, dragging one foot, weary and sick. I doubt that he could be persuaded to honor what others do. Deprived of rapture in a darkened universe, stripped of hope, he compared mortals to insentient insects which at the penultimate hour of life develop wings. As for evidence he cited none. Once I heard him say the Lion tawny with pride stands immaculate against the light, resplendent in gold. But of proof? Cetera desunt.

DISCIPLES he taught to examine Mercaba's blistering chariot, the magnet of Helvetius, Aupuleius' midnight moon— binding moral geography with foolish dreams. Let us extract from the rampant King rose-colored blood, from the ascendant Queen pale gluten that we might display the stone inscribed Tinctura Physicorum! Thus he skipped about lecturing, raving. Yet no likeness of himself did he bring to Cardan. Fomalhaut does not pronounce his fame nor will those resonant treatises find their way to ladies' tables. Mayhap he thought it best to speak on the birthplace of Scolopendra, of how camer-

ith burns, the flavor of Man, vapors and effluxions and aliment and the indelible colors of Egypt, of saxatilic spirits and six corners of the universe. On so much he chose to expound in lieu of court etiquette. Perhaps, like meat in the belly, life had lost its taste.

𝕴 HEARD him discourse on a pilgrim to Santiago de Compostela that had a great Bell cast from electrum out of which swarmed Apparitions which hurried to obey him when he rang this bell. Divers creatures stood forth—ghosts, animals and flying fish came attracted to the sound—but as not so many were employed this sorcerer dispersed them by uttering blasphemous syllables. In my judgment the master grew rapt with thaumaturgic allegory. I suspect he was born at eight months.

𝕳E SAID that instruction rings more agreeably than silver, wisdom weighs more heavily than gold, and this world is but a materiate transcript of some invisible pattern fabricated by God to recapitulate His spiritual universe—that we might altogether comprehend His teaching. And thus we watch heaven reflected in nature as though we watched it through a looking-glass. And so we pursue alchymic science not for mineral wealth but for the acquisition of knowledge, being always vigilant, quick to falsify or dissimulate lest prodigious mysteries be considered by insignificant men that might look upon our revelations with illiterate contempt. Magians from the past such as Porphyry, Pythagoras, Orpheus, Plato and the Cabalists—did they not enjoin mystification? Did not Jesus disguise truth with parable? But what counsel does such inquiry make? I am divided by doubt. Toward midnight did the master expose clawed hands?

That he knew the constituents of the Philosopher's Stone seems undeniable, describing it as unlike rough stone nor any sort of gamaheus, except by puissant resistance to the activities of fire. All claim it resembles gold—inconceivably pure gold—being simultaneously immanent and incombustible with a delicate aspect. Neither gypsum nor galena nor hematite nor malachite nor potash nor alum nor sulfur nor any recognizable element may be detected, because it is sweet to the taste and indwelling, fragrant and unctuous and positive, therefore it must be fundamental. Many define it as consensitive with art, spiritual, tenuous, penetrative, indissolubly restorative, by such virtues urging lesser metals toward consummation. Yet to say of it that it is materiate or incorporate would negate its value. Except for a human soul the Stone appears our noblest agent of restitution, which is why at the time of this beneficence all mankind shall clap hands in unison. So said the master. But the days of hermetic chymists are differently reckoned, being more or less than common days.

I think he considered the monarchy of the mind to be his—pretending he never praised himself, although nature did because he was born of her and followed her directorate. He said we visit twelve ineffable cities, nevertheless no place belongs to us. Small use had I for such a tumbling cataract of mystification. Arrogance seemed his watchword. He said there lay buried at Friaul a topaz so rich that neither Carolus nor Leo could buy it despite their wealth. From his perch on a bird-limed twig he declaimed, scourging mankind, racked by his obligation to testify. Ex abundantia cordis os loquitur.

HE SPOKE of Umbratiles which are but distant shadows grown tangible, and of primary spirits—Xeni Nephidei which bite and guzzle the brains of men. He inquired if salvation may be had through fasting or lip-prayer, if beatings and black drapes be good, or if it be true that upon the dung marsh of hypocrisy faith flourishes. I thought he boasted over-much. Being taken by himself he neglected to distinguish rectitude from the dignity of ideals. In my opinion he regarded the title Heretic a stamp of honor—if truth begins as heresy.

NEITHER titles nor eloquence do we require, he said, nor an insidious tongue nor familiarity with saffron myths on painted scrolls, but patience to disengage difficulties until matters disclose their essence without opposition, because the most subtle understanding outweighs mountains.

TO THE commonest argument of life he seemed indifferent. Years of reflective solitude had so disordered him that often-times when he spoke he made meager sense—stumbling, hesitating—as if that valedictory elocution habitual to pedagogues conflicted with the repository of his mind. I have heard him compared to a man born in the Dark Ages for those cunning perceptions of life—anxious, lacerated. But I judged him renascent because of his high conviction that we were meant to engender something new.

ℕEVER did I see him submit to idleness or stroll about lost in a proud cloak, wearing plush and gray velvet with Moresque rings circling both thumbs, and gloves, while a dagger jiggled at his thigh, but he would labor diligently, and at night he sweated beside the furnace instead of promenading. And he wore a leathern garment with a pouch, with an apron foul as the devil's arse, thrusting his fingers into horse dung, coal and lute, surprising us not with emeralds. He was a dirty man. Black as a blacksmith or collier, sooty in countenance, reeking full of scales, he did not gossip to patients and vaunt feeble remedies but swore the work glorified the workman, not vice-versa. Swollen tight with vanity he would pump his ancient bellows to undertake the magisterial yet tenebrous concept of reverberation, putrefaction, extraction, calcination, final projection, reduction and the like. None came to touch this vagrant insensible to muddy craving, estranged by some immortal curse. I never heard him laugh.

𝔸 VARIETY of little pills in aspect and color and size resembling mouse turds he concocted which were Opium—called after the name of a white medicament locked in the pommel of his sword, which he would prescribe for dysentery, spasm, night-walking, excrescence and similar complaints. Fame of a sort accompanied such treatment, but I suspect the voyage on which he embarked meant little to esurient apprentices. And that any physician should foist doubtful analeptics upon suffering patients caused medicasters to vilify him for contravening established usage. On account of this, I believe, whenever the unremitting progress of loathsome disease yielded to his magistery like the morning star acceding to daylight—noting as much, they despised him and crept about whispering how he was a greasy castrate fornicating with cacodemons past midnight and therefore he should be strangled. The word Azoth he had engraved on his great flat sword—a synonym for Mercurius which is the sovereign panacea gathering strength from others, Alpha to Omega.

I HEAR of knotted ecclesiarchs who charge him for submission and obeisance to Lucifer's command with the aid of mineral fire—which may be. Also, it is said he fathered an homunculus without the cooperation of a woman. That he visited Byzantium on his journey to converse with infidels and purchase secrets goes unquestioned. I am told he gave orders on his deathbed that his body be quartered and buried with manure. Afterward, as it was exhumed, the parts miraculously had grown together and I have heard that but for the nervousness of a disciple hurrying to complete this wicked rite the master would have awakened. I do not know. I am sure only that had I listened further to the torrent of his mind I would be lost.

THIS world he compared to a distillatory moulded by two hands upon which prototype physicians model alembics whose purpose is similar—healing and synopsis. I think he was borne past the frame of things. In my judgment the shadows of his mind traveled farther than himself.

HE WOULD have us composed of two forms, one from the earth and one derived from the universe. He said the first, being elemental, subsides and divellicates, whereas the celestial flows back subtly toward its source, as the spirit happily returns to Him whose image it was. Therefore each chooses that medium from whence it issued. So, I think, do we fail to perceive but become a thing perceived. By some such path does light gain access to the soul.

HE SAID that we partake of ourselves as one envisaging Gold approximates its essence, or imagining Fire calls up himself toward revenge. And so we are sustained among discrepancies since the probity of our meditations cannot be disregarded. But is an end more than its commencement displayed, manifest and wrought out? For if not, then the end must be generated among obscure beginnings.

I PROPOSED that if we do not enter into an understanding of ourselves, and of those fallibilities which enchant us, how should we explain what is meant by a theology of Fall and Regeneration, or presume to liberate ignoble substance from its original curse? Attila, Theodoric, and the tyrant of Padua, Ezzelino de Romano, gained strength from Satan's loins, just as Cain was born to Eve by a visiting incubus. If he heard, I know not. He answered by saying that mortal and immortal things never were intended to embrace nor touch nor dwell together.

DOES perfection express itself as unity? Beneath what shape shall we cast off malice? If sulfur should represent nature is the supernatural evoked by mercury? What is burning Sol but the infinite conservatory of man? How are five imperfect minerals transmuted? Iron, copper, tin, lead, quicksilver—how are they reconstituted? What alters them into alchymic gold? Lacking the breath of divinity, where do we separate good from evil? I do not know. Having studied without hope or resolution or faith, I approached the master who replied that out of all created subjects we have declared ourselves epitome, believing we were meant to secure universalities so that we would not confound things with their neighbors—because we grow toward completion externally. And for this we should anticipate no recourse since we were designated microcosm which carries heaven from its onset. And he said that because of abhorrent acts men commit there is savagery about the Lord. But fidelity cannot be divided or mixed.

HOW shall we be distinguished from Cain who was driven out of a society he once enjoyed, tossed by unconscionable wind forward and backward, imperiled at every pause? Do we not lament and weep and groan and complain upward to providence while journeying through merciless kingdoms? Or in counting our possessions do we not wonder that superior texts teach opacities? Or how should extremities be joined, except by medians? Or what man was born free while enslaved to flesh? Indolent students would lap up truth at once, he said, like dogs filling their bellies from the Rhine.

BEING asked if knowledge may controvert metaphysic, he said that the former can be but a digest of experience—threads drawn to various aspects. And while our Lord God has resolved to hide many things from us, they must at last be discovered since we are born with a rage to know.

How could the fabric of theology be woven in a day? Learning deploys from loom to loom, he said, out of Byzantium and Syria to Latinate Europe, therefore mutuality is guaranteed. Enigma precedes enigma.

How is it that private magic inhabits all? Flint must hold some fiery essence or spirit because sparks appear, jubilant with motion. But why? From nine every morning until mid-day what makes the chickweed flower upright? Following the rain what makes it pendant? How do we gain by seeing gold branch within the retort? Are we left much wiser than before? Still we must ask the name of a water that does not wet the hand, identify the wingless bird, decipher messages whitely written on stone. So a promise stands before our eyes. Ante oculos stabat quidquid promiserat annus.

WE HAVE watched the pelican feed her offspring new blood drawn from herself by angrily pecking at her own breast—the nacreous parent providing sustenance for its young. We observe the monarch delivering himself of vile matter, base, foul, dust and spittle, matter overlooked, divers powder. How is this? Rigorous inquiries oblige us to dream no less than Mikoiaj Kopernik's drawing set heaven ablaze with heresy impossible to extinguish. Does harmony result from the analogy of opposites? Our thoughts dart and rush like haddock swarming in springtime that surge to and fro. We wonder how God—if He is an incomprehensible, infinite, eternal light—should manifest His presence to the world except as light.

METALS which burn and give up harmoniac to the aether become calx, yet their metallic virtues will reappear if charcoal containing sufficient harmoniac is supplied. Hence we understand how iron rusts, because what is rust except iron from which atomic consonance was extracted? What is salvation but man rescued from obliquity?

WHY should moss accumulating on the skull of a corpse acquire magnetic strength exceeding that of vegetables and herbs? Because wisdom steadily flows from mummial marrow, because mankind first held the seed of heaven. Thus the skull's shape must be our universe reproduced in miniature, diminished by suffering. To what purpose then do we overlook that rare conjunction, trafficking in useless wealth from star to star?

DO FRAGILE particles grow agitated by our proximity? I believe they do because not one of us exists alone, so all objects must be subject to another's posture. Then, as now, we are tied up with reciprocal currents. Yet if we were intended to embrace the moon, the sun, the planets and migrant stars, why should we embrace chaos within?

PROBLEMS try the intelligence. Through prismatic crystal I have directed beams of sunlight, marveling ignorantly at the result since the proximity of light's vital elixir eludes the most ingenious box built to catch its animus. I feel troubled and dismayed by such compulsive liberty. I find many things that transpire below are but a diurnal reflection of majesties overhead. Now my left eye, being secular, cagastric, carnal, I will close and keep closed while my other eye, being iliastric, looks to eternity. But is this wise? If imagination turns wherever I want, how should the course of my gaze be altered?

GRANTED the administration of our Lord, why am I distraught? Deo adjuvante, non timendum. Divinity burgeons in the heart. What is gold if not an itinerant ray of sunlight solidified? I have seen how sunshine acts against the earth, compounding metals until they sprout like crocus since everything below obtains sustenance from above. Have not diamonds multiplied in long-abandoned pits? Hence we look downward to fertility in an underground kingdom, to eternal life painting the dust. I perceive in this a mysterious arrangement of logic, albeit I know not the method. I labor at holy questions.

I HAVE seen the fecund seed separate and divide itself, disintegrating, dissolving, renouncing its existence to provide a nutritious matrix for the growing plant. Does this argue that corruption leads to fulfillment? I am bound by a circumference of mystery.

WITH what gratitude we look upward from ordure in the street to the glory of cathedrals, yet why is not the opposite true? Where does the dominion of conscience fall? I would inquire, but every question leads to another more paradoxical, more tenebrous. Bernard de Clairvaux, governed by his respect for the universe, sought refuge in contemplative restrictions. Anticipating guidance, I wait. I think the mind is embryonic, accumulating strength while it seeks perfection.

DAME Hildegard has extolled humanity's deeds for influencing celestial light while the master speaks of stellar excrement that illuminates summer evenings. Nevertheless, both define the truth as a fertilized egg. How is it that both disregard the issue? Is not the body woven of starlight? Are we conceived in water only to rise screaming against the air? I see no deliverance outside the Church. Extra ecclesiam nulla salus.

NOTHING exists that was not a consideration of our Lord, said the master, but I am weary of mysteries, of spirals. I am weary from gathering them in, I am sick. I am unsure what to think. I cannot climb up to heaven, I grow afraid of the South Sea. I know not what I am.

SUPPOSE the royalty I invoke is but some sliding element, then is the universe unstable? Should a tree overflowing with fertility provide shade for pilgrims? Is transient good sufficient? How did the allegoric labor of Hercules fulfill philosophy's secret? Were not Helen born to Venus would she yet be a whore? Does the moon engender lunatics? Is not the avowed purpose of each hierophant to fabricate ultimate metal from blemished, penultimate matter? Adepts proliferate, plants decay. Demons meddle beneath the glory of provocative constellations and I am but a simple novice drowning. Still I praise God.

WATER disperses across the multi-colored surface of earth, it takes up the hue and flavor of that area where it rests. So does man absorb his fundament and neglects to distinguish each thing from the next—awarding to multitudinous items equivocal shape or latitude, like a poor navigator unable to descry safe land who foolishly persists against the rim, content with one expanse.

OUR eyes we trust to describe what we see, our ears to interpret noise, while lesser senses similarly enact their part. Nonetheless what was heard or seen, or otherwise apprehended, must prove erroneous because we rule mistakenly. Even as the testament of Thesaurus Philosophiae declares, what we would consider self-evident is but a malicious distortion so that we grovel and writhe through perpetual darkness, indifferent to heaven except as it rains or blows.

HAVE we been so registered that we must twist and complain, riveled of understanding, equivalent to beasts that perish ignorant? Blessed we call those resident mercuries of occult and imperial craft since without them we would be restricted to shallow sensitivities. Therefore the Jew, Philo, explains how God presides above mortal cogitation as though He dwelt in a palace. Dixit et facta sunt.

Through stages of flux we plummet—dizzily revolving corks that whirl around a watery vortex—incapable of resisting our own volition yet quick and anxious to explain anagrams secured within the closet of matter, redefining symmetries that are but the meanest crust of nature. Thus has Vaughan, the Welshman, decried humanity as presumptuous or ludicrous for attempting to weigh jewels concealed in a cabinet.

Valentinus asks what are the circumstances of a thing, considering both form and matter, if neither principle nor ambience may be gathered except by rigorous trial. Yet what could be more ostentatious, more vainglorious than subjecting God's counsel to doubt? His dimensions, being infinite, can be comprehended by our Lord alone. But I am a neophyte with moderate understanding, adrift on a limitless ocean.

Eirenaeus would have us grasp and plunge into bottomless quicksilver that which simulates gold, whose centrality cannot be revealed either below or above save by its own revelation— which I take for the center rising everywhere whose circumference bends the light. This seems admirable, implying still higher perfection.

PLOTINUS asks how we should conceive of the illimitable. What is its idiom? How might such an image be entertained without unreason? Accordingly did he investigate himself as one among the order of beings—this reality attested by his reminiscence. Isolated by the unyielding strength of intellectual resolve from externals, gently subsiding toward the deeps of mortal rectitude, he enabled himself to apprehend a most commendable beauty and became certain that the matter of his life was excellent, more specific, more cognizant than that of trees and fishes. So to this without intermission he directed his thought.

I ASK myself if there be unequivocal truths for humanity, just as with animals a single leader is selected to reign undisputed and as the kingly sun would repudiate a rival. I think it must be the provenance of intellect to decide by adjudication which verities to clasp, which to reject, among the plenitude of falsehoods. Is not mystery round and close? Are not men eversible, predestined to off-set obnubilities? Yet are they favored with holy bones?

I HAVE thought on how Man loiters outside wisdom's vestibule when I behold him chart progressions from privacy to acclaim, out of mineral accomplishment to diurnal usage—as do Turks that aspire to Paradise fall tumbling in the muck with hogs. Praise be to God, we grasp the glittering sword of knowledge to split asunder our philosophic Egg and disclose the matrix where prominent metals achieve their maturities among rock. We watch cinnabar grow into lead, graduating next to silver and continuing upward to fulfillment. So do all in extremis disclose their ambition. All speak with a loud voice.

Does the mind seize opportunities according to its purpose? Betimes have I met chymists ready to jest at transmutation, but they do not answer when asked to justify vitreous logs or petrified forests. Narrow clerics and such-like chymists I abhor, that nigrify a realm with prejudice. If the flesh and blood of Jesus Christ manifests itself out of substance like bread and wine, metallic reformation seems inevitable. If one element acquires new form, what prohibits the rest?

Louts and fools and rustics may jeer at the hierophantic language of metaphysicians or denounce occult pharmacies as some crippled science because, lacking true guidance, they think such learning inconceivable. So do they mock Lingua Adamica which is the language all servants of God understand, by which they are summoned. So does gnostic fortune ebb or flow. How could the wisest proceed upward if not through transcendental art?

We have been taught that when a man travels with darkness he need not feel despair, no more than one bathed in light, because both shall advance according to their preference. And there is a wheel which God directs or keeps in motion by multifarious signs while comets upon intersecting courses conspire to notify men of the future, although their paths diverge. Te Deum laudamus.

No doubt we wander apart from inclinations, imagining our lives as furnaces of empyrean flame both incorruptible and inextinguishable whose virtuosity flows from the spirit, therefore what is annealed must be empty in the marketplace. Van Suchten reminds us of how novices that lust toward gold will pollute their senses by coveting what none can acquire, which means that our least hope of satisfaction is illusory.

I know that the highest mountain will be that which rests upon the deepest fundament, thus each alchymic novitiate looks to exceeding subventions. And since he was awarded this middle position between earth and heaven, so must he secure the best ground of hope for humanity's development from a limited estate to one more exalted. Now, it is clear that from an onion sprout we do not harvest an apricot nor a walnut nor a cabbage head, nor anything except an onion. Thus we look to uncoagulate gold—which we call the habitat of mercury. Ecce signum.

Without understanding we know what we seek. Allegories perfect in rectitude, Christian oracles, dew from the point of a leaf. Thus do we enter the Castle to advise pilgrims on their quest, denounce false prophecy, persevere at sublimation, encourage dead trees to flower—declaring our great search with parable or sign. So by this jointure would we reconstitute those seven immaculate circles of Paradise.

We would not adopt the Devil's black-on-yellow livery nor commit evil on roof-tops. Threats, laments, cries of murder or abuse of any sort—this does but encourage our easement.

Crippling punishment, censure—so much seems our messuage since what has been destined for superiority comes dressed in misreport. And all notice of accomplishment we withhold until a propitious instant, lest we dissipate our office with faint hope of restitution.

Nothing do we covet save the ineffable distillate of radiance achieved through multiplication of the subtle from the gross. Yet we do not divulge our procedure, which would be illogical since hieratic knowledge acquired by the obtuse or insensate could not benefit our holding. This wealth that we accumulate was intended to remain perpetually indescribable and ethically incommunicable. Enlightenment should be kept from avaricious sellers or buyers, knavish mercenaries that hope to mortgage humanity's consignment. Why? Because no dividend shall accrue by distributing hermetic valuables. Were such administration advised, all is lost. Instead, we provide mystic instruction ornamented by allusion and augury and metaphor. Why is this? Because of a world we find enwrapped with obscurity. Dominus illuminatio mea.

We have been taught how endless rivers do not fill to the lip a bottomless bowl, nor should perishable teachers anticipate immortality. Hence, we disregard gasconades of expectation and wait on the presiding animus within, laboring to complete that craft which common chymists leave unfulfilled. The seed prefiguring regeneration would we withdraw out of base lead. Granted the beneplacit of our God, shall not morning be made but evening also?

SINCE man is Executive, epitome of the universe, encompassing within his spirit every principality and kingdom, we consider all things feasible. So we look to man as the supreme retort, an alembic, a cucurbit within which fermentation will occur and thoughts be distilled. Accordingly we mean to crystallize, to dissolve and to ferment and convert, to project, to purify. Thus the first step is calefaction of dross whereby we elevate lead toward that fulfillment which proceeds from annihilation of the self. And this may be achieved with the aid of remedial art so long as man governs the earth, however limited his body, which is why we look to each meridian.

TO THE apprentice disavowing telluric life through malice or indifference, no success is conceivable. Nor should talent compensate for one that hesitates while regenerating his soul. Truly are we advised by the philosophist to extract and hold within a cup that rare tincture, since at length it is given provided the supplicant prove worthy. But if we would succumb to false magistery, thirst or blindness may ensue. Adamantine walls separate Neophyte from Adept and roiling seas intervene, lest a novice set foot on iridescent sand.

WOULD a man who owned a goose agree to pluck it and cook it, hold it up to his neighbor's teeth and wipe away the grease? Assuredly not. Then what alchymist should encourage the lame or lead the blind? We think no seminarian depending openly on his senses was meant to profit from the puissant magistery of intuitive art, a subject wise men considered too precious for public expenditure. Nor is there benefit for sectarians, idolators, fanatics or dilettantes. Adepts avow that ancient riddles become two-edged instruments which carve out dainties for reverent initiates, yet slash the thumbs of greedy fools. Are not our lives varied and manifold and mightily surpassing measurement? Truly does Horatius say we have not been ordered to know everything. Nec scire fas est omnia.

PERFECT apprehension of mortal affairs was not bequeathed us since the objects of our sublunary world continually change. Yet I think all concepts and substances must be harmoniously balanced. How else could we justify pyramids of office and of class and of rank? By itself every microcosm responds for an entirety, which enables us to cross toward the next. Matters interweave to separate afresh, blooming, flowering, commingling, mixed and unmixed. Why should not the lectern become an altar?

IF, AS we are taught, the earth was but recently formed, Man must be incomplete, destined to undergo three metamorphoses. Accordingly each neophyte seeks his place on the Catena Aurea, that resplendent chain of metaphysical theosophers descending from Ianna the Mesopotamian to Orpheus, Persephone, Odysseus and to our Lord. But what of myself? What of me, Lord Jesus? When shall I behold the tutelary angel? Swollen with desire yet denied Thy privilege, I become arrogant in my dejection. Still I look up to the high vault of Christianity.

I TAKE the cross surmounted by the rose to be the heraldic device of heretics, therefore Rosicrucians must be disciples of Martin Luther despatched to promulgate this most noxious and abominable faith. Abbé Gaultier has preached the subject. I wonder that men crouch behind such palisades of ignorance. Mounted upon lame donkeys they go galloping after the wind. Their spirits must be twisted, lapped in lead, dry cordage. See them flutter over books. Some believe the teeth of Jesus Christ were exhibited in Jerusalem beside a thumb of the Holy Ghost, a phial of St. Michael's sweat, a gleam from that star followed by three Orient kings to Bethlehem. How are men induced, age after age, to confirm and reiterate unspeakable falsehood? I myself ask not where heaven stands. How could I demand the presence of my Lord?

BECAUSE everything flows toward us from a single fountain with each compounded of primordial essence, it must follow that all stand related—all must be conjoined materially and spiritually, while dissimilarities that possibly exist or appear to exist between animate and inanimate entities must result from divergent growth. Yet where is the cause of ontogeny? Bernardino Telesio encourages us to inquire not through recapitulating sterile argument but employing the logical use of natural senses toward our surrounding—if heaven and earth be half-synonymous. And that being so, what choice have men but to praise their benefactor? Tullus Hostilius spurned his gods, only to recant when distraught. I wonder how God contrives to love those abjuring faith.

THROUGH meditation would we become visible confidants of God, of involute mystery proceeding not from evident impressions, as we have seen the astral spirits of leaves brought to life out of ashes, so in time we may be likened to Christian apostles. And therefore I think that with the highest causes some exuberance of power must be present, just as the mystic transfiguration of a silk-worm holds within some enlistment to baffle reason, diverting the mind of an observer from philosophy to divinity.

PROVIDENCE supplies our refuge, it provides a sanctuary upon which we depend, guiding our thought past egregious misapprehension by directing us gently toward the house of our Creator, to whom we appeal like thirsting animals gathered by the mighty dispensation of a limitless ocean. Yet how should the sweet blessing of divinity be limited to a restricted universe? Is not the eye of God attentive to His inimitable work? Was not all intuitively foreseen by an omniscient workman who makes no mistake? Pythagoras endeavors to persuade us how the earth resembles a planet similar to the moon where infinite mercy rules by virtue of which things frame their environment, holding shadows or vestiges or traces of indecipherable nature. I myself travel crookedly, questioning much. How can it be with men that no two lift similar prayers?

DO WE not hang and tremble upon the hour? Yet in all things have we found theology, though the heart be mailed with oak and bronze and we have admired fruit pendulous on the bough. I believe holy indulgence coincides with mortal aspiration since we do not mount to heaven by a ladder, but we inquire and ask what should be resolved while the penitent abstains from dreaming, while the river slides and rolls.

$\mathfrak{W}$HAT is more prophetic than lost equilibrium? I have seen gold branch within the aludel. I have watched the Princess wearing a coronet of foliage squeeze milk from her breast to nourish our Regal Infant. And I have observed the Elder approach. Like a dilatory Franciscan that would lie abed while his brothers' scythes sweep back and forth to gather a ripening harvest, so have I lain wrapped in conjuration. Apparitions vanish, strange fictions imprint their image upon a heart without consent. Therefore do I gaze upward to my shelter, my refuge. When shall I visit the heavenly city of Sarras?

$\mathfrak{H}$OW should one request admittance by that alabaster gate were he not refashioned? Alchymic masters teach that with a purification of Gold we imply mankind regenerate. Silver, although it is precious and able to resist fire, undergoes less evolution, hence it is subject to corrosion by sulphur or nitric acid—which explains why we liken this rare metal to regenerate humanity at its lowest period of development. Dull and ponderous Lead depicts the unregenerate.

$\mathfrak{L}$ET us say natural forces could realign mercury with sulphur to make new minerals, then why could not magisterial artists duplicate such feats of transmutation within their alembics? Similarly, the mind and body of man consisting of loathsome effluent would shrivel, corrode and turn black—reappearing anew, incorruptible as gold. But we may no more expect a man to be what he is not than we may direct a pine to be an elm or copper to be silver, not unless both have been subducted to the quintessence which we know as Protyle. And upon this consanguinity we teach the mystical resurrection of Osiris, of Buddha, of our Christian Lord.

As THE chip of Lodestone suggests perfection across two poles, so does every spark of fire embrace the generating principle of its elements, thus fragments of existence proportionately live continent and fulfilled. Just as a man united with God becomes divinely empowered, at liberty to act or to meditate as he chooses, being no more than a palimpsest of his deity in consonance with reason, similarly our Stone appropriates to itself the imperial task of transmutation from what it was into what it promises. At that hour shall Mankind stand forth to the Antipodes burnished with truth, surpassing excellence. Ultima Thule shall prove no limit and stars take up positions as they did when the world unrolled. And I am content to wait and praise the interior shape of things—vapor virtutis Dei, Ruach Elohim—which brooded over the face of waters.

It IS true that I am a poor novitiate and truly is my faith compared to a Hammer. So does my faith resound. So do I labor to defeat the sightless figure inhabiting my cell, struggling against duality. Nineteen years have I fought without success against myself. Like the creature Ourobouros annulling itself as circles round, I am become too young for death. Therefore I ask why shapes are sacrificed to resurrection more valuable than at their beginning, since the center is a circumference toward which all journeys tend.

Who knocks? Who? Some novice wearing a black skull-cap to hide both ears cropped in the pillory for coinage? Some lapsed or untidy pilgrim that digged up a corpse by Walton-le-Dale and stole to practice his necromantic art? From the plenitude of human souls I would inquire how many are not deformed.

Rumors of a wandering magus conceived in heresy . . .

$\mathfrak{F}$ROM Scotland to grimy England, from Portugal to Bohemia, from muddy Palestine to Germany pseudo-alchymists quarrel, boasting stupendous effects even as they pump the bellows. O yea! And we have met imposters more agile than roaches, desirous as Frenchmen hawking fragrant packets of crystal drenched with rose-water. But of that Great Magisterium—glistering, saffron-colored, faultless—slender evidence. Like some harsh powder brought from India or liquid resin exuded out of evergreens, iridescent while opaque, pliant yet more frangible than glass, simultaneously transparent, nacrous and malleable, it bathes in the light of planets by whose jurisdiction imperfections change.

$\mathfrak{W}$E DOUBT that gold-weighted quartz responds to a quivering rod, or that precipitate milked from macerated butterflies spontaneously glows at midnight. Victims of abundant phlegm, does heavy rain inundate their dreams? We suspect not. Also, we doubt Sendivogius for asserting that concentrated bismuth expands beneath the rising moon. Indeed, sophistical rhetoric floats on the surface of our craft like froth upon fresh wine. Much we find gilded, varnished and bundled up in gaudy tissue flecked with mica to deceive the ignorant.

Or, WE have been advised that in Egypt lives a rare bird yclept Ibis which walks up to stroke the Crocodile with its feathers so the monster squats paralyzed. And gossip of one that rises chittering to fly off when it sees the Horse. We hear further about a prodigious stone named Magnes brought over to Europe from an Eastern Isle which can know if a man's wife be chaste, since when it is thrust underneath her pillow while she sleeps if she has been faithful she will begin efforts to embrace him, but if not she must kick at her husband and cause difficulty. Also, we have heard much about wonderful jugglers from India that have perfected the queer deceptive art for gathering up and applying formulas which make shrubs spring out of soil by manipulation through evocative gestures with their hands, but how they accomplish this Magic escapes our understanding. Yea, we do give ourselves to false prophets dictating marvels like fox-hounds that yelp after false echoes. Meister Archytus would remind us how discoveries materialize with ease to those that explore rightly, so how should a man control any substance unless by fixed attention to its behavior he deduce its law.

Have we not found copper counterfeited by varnishing iron with laminar malachite? Indeed. Likewise we simulate gold by obducting silver with white of egg. Surfaces heighten, true, but what endures cannot be subtracted. Accordingly we meddle with nothing out of kind, be this sulfur or salt or anything of such imposition. To the inimitable elixir alien matter appears reprobate. Do not dissemble by deceit nor misleading discourse.

Now what? This Muslim yclept Rhases, born Abu Bakr Muhammad ibn Zakariyya, explains how quasi-physicians root out snakes from a patient's nose by thrusting into the nostril a gilded probe to bring forth blood with a dead worm of sliced liver. And they know how to draw water from an ear and slimy insects from teeth—O, they do this! Aye! And they will wring mucus out of interior body parts and draw up great bladder-stones, all having shifted by their hands that which they pretend to extract. Who would believe such a thing?

We avow by man's hindpart we have met talkative swindlers willing to traffic in posteriority for a moment's wealth, charlatans that make up sparkling pyramids instead of funding ancient verities—mischievous spirits that choose to engage innocents with error by undermining the edifice of sound philosophy. So the earth whirls and rings about us to make its great noise, yet planting-time and harvest time have each their due return.

Lo! What next? An erudite Jesuit by name Athanasius Kircher notifies us how some Stranger visiting a youthful aspirant at his workshop dictated the recipe we seek! And graciously did he labor to help produce a congealing Oil that forthwith separated, reducing itself to dust while swiftly converting three hundred pounds of quicksilver into fresh hermetic gold which could not through any test be adulterated or subdued—whereupon this benefactor departed, albeit we know not why. Then did our novice experience ambitious pains like midnight with a vacant bellie and set out to recapitulate the process. O yea! Woe! Since next we hear he delivered up his inheritance to questionable art. Were not men hatched from unlucky eggs? And among us how many are not insidiously nudged or buggered by that Advocate who takes such joy in blurring and smearing and contaminating sublunary affairs?

RICALMUS prepares us his catalogue of farts and stratagems practiced upon the unwary by satanic agents with dishonest gestures and seductive appointments. O, it is true! Vipers lurk betwixt and behind green leaves. Hence are we reminded that as the bewitching vagabond appears most innocent, there should we walk most circumspect.

MAGISTER Solomon Trismosin discourses in Aureum Vellus how he encountered this wizard of secretive temperament that called himself Flocker and used a measure of lead fixed with brimstone to make it first rigid, then fluid, at last turning the metal soft as wax, and so contrived to draw out eight ounces of excellent silver. Afterward said Flocker went tumbling down a mine-shaft leaving for his legacy manifold notes and regrets, but about the process not much. So little develops by chance while too much exhibited as sacrosanct we mistrustfully deride, even as we suspect our Moon does not sail east—although clouds rush westward across her smiling visage. Well, Anno Domini 1598 from Rorschach comes a most grave manuscript alleging that by fortune's grace our Solomon fell heir to Flocker's heroic recipe and betook himself in travel about Asia where he was identified centuries later! O, mercy! Could Solomon live so long? We think not. Much we dispute, more we doubt. Perjuries blow off the wind, sapphires suck poison out of tumors, and as comets oppose their tails to the Sun we do grow evasive against majorities.

Magister Anselm Boetius de Boodt proposes the regeneration of earth into a Jewel by virtue of its lapidific endowment, agitated and urged toward movement through celestial warmth, during which a conclusive role was performed by the Lord—Deus Optimus Maximus. Ach! Our brain feels ploughed in wrinkles. We doubt if Borri with his palm-branch might sweep the court of such a smelly pie. Nor, saying so, would we disparage God, but donkeys that invest his pasture.

Wonder has seized us regarding this manuscript Sarlamethon that was purchased by a gullible Italian for three thousand crowns. Then what? Up from Hades bubbled an Adriatic storm so our greedy Latin with his gold pass-port sank from view. Yea! O, what a pitiful story! Is the Adriatic at mid-winter less raging or turbulent than mankind? Do we not all swarm with vague or mixed anxieties? Meister Albertus in his silly Book of Secrets affirms how travel across distant countries wearies us, yet Eirenaeus Philalethes cautions that the ignorant are consigned to frantic struggles in endless thickets. Truly, we respond like buckets on a rope—as one goes up his brother falls. Thus we consult the mist and contend at morality, asking if this be autumn or summer but do not guess what sign old Sol held.

WE ARE told in Philostratus Jarchus that some Hindoo prince bequeathed seven rings with the seven signatures of regnant planets to Apollonius, who vowed to wear them sequentially and by such magic live beyond one hundred years, yet retain the comeliness of youth. But do we not hear about the Bear that after five centuries he becomes a Fox? So among Wolves which after eight hundred birthdays select different shapes. Verily! Thus might oceans roil overhead—as Patricius claims. So do rats foretelling human events turn white. So do smoaky exhalations ascending from putrid matter inside the stomach suffocate the intellect.

MUCH gossip patters on our heads regarding two fleet wizards from Elizabeth's Court by name John Dee—appointed warden of Manchester College—with his accomplice Kelley that in a ruin near Glastonbury uncovered a Liquid which they took with them all across the Continent so far as Trebona, there performing a little hermetic music to multiply their fortune. Moreover, we hear of one Sendivogius traveling disguised like a lackey with a box of magic powder tucked in his waistcoat— one pinch sufficient to project ducats out of mercury ounce for ounce! And we do affirm how mortal existence appears a concatenation of days linking absurdity to absurdity.

𝕹ow are we notified how at the residence of Thaddeus de Hazek—Imperial Medicaster—our English Kelley did manage to extract from quick-silver one full pound of gold, diluting the matrix with a quiddity so estimable that following this transmutation some jewel similar to a Ruby manifested itself upon the slag, a miracle devoutly attested by that most virtuous physician, Doctor Nicholas Barnaud. Whereupon our illustrious sovereign Maximilian skipped merrily off the saddle to welcome this foreign cock's-broth at Court and knighted and anointed him Grand Marshal of Bohemia! But concerning the actual worth of such unworthiness, does a silver circle plugged in a hog's snout enrich his carcass? Alchymists contend of their subject that it is Man—not legerdemain toward the benefits of office. And this saltimbank that was born blagueur, canter, Pharisee, fabulist, romancer, taradiddle, Ananias, cockatrice—plus we know not what greater jilt—having lost both ears for untold mischief, concealed the disgrace beneath a snug velvet bonnet to give his features a most oracular and thoughtful appearance. O, we are familiar with the bulk of them from Jean de Gallans to Georges Sabellicus, from Guy de Crusembourg to Wenzel von Reinburg, from Domenico Caetano to the mysterious Richtausen. Aye! Lincture and tincture and wax and one stuffed crocodile, so much have we met and guess times present do but iterate upon our proscenium things past.

𝖁ARIOUS honest scholars have certified to the fly-trap skill and crafty jugglement at laudable science of Arnold di Villa Nova. John André, Jurisconsult, once observed this mountebank in Rome sub-ducting gold from iron bars. Nevertheless, facts vary at the circumference, presumptions collapse, perimeters dissolve. Vapors darken the alembic. Alain de l'Isle distilled the Magisterium, we hear, but we hear also that brute savages in thatch huts beyond the Western Sea have netted the wily Scolopendra! Well, from the credulous we do not withhold credulity, placing much value on firm belief. Is not theriac prescribed for melodious dreams? May not the flesh of winged dragons alleviate bloody flux? Or catechitic instruction by demons—is not that preferable to ignorance?

𝕿OWARD every uncommon triumph do we wax fulsome with praise. O yea! High homage therefore to Ramon Lull that did persuade King Edward on how to lubricate his crusade, thus acquiring as work-shop a drafty chamber of the fabulous Tower. What next? Presto! Twenty-three English tons of quicksilver turned sombresault into gold as pliant as that which informs a Jacobus! Aye! And medals were coined from this bounteous slag-heap by Edward's order whose purity exceeds description, which men have labeled Rose Nobles. Was not this marvelous? We exclaim at such merit yet ask how Rose Nobles be weighed, if currencies be but simulacra and durable shades of life.

𝕿RULY, much homage do we render this numinous philosopher that has built a Machine of concentric disks which revolve about an Axis in order to convert Mahometans. Upon its rim sixteen chambers interlock and each proclaims his message: Philosophy, Virtue, Justice, Dominion, Humility, Magnitude, and the rest, whereby innumerable combinations are secured. So did Hermes Trismegistus construct the city of Adocentyn whose light-house sequentially flashed the hues of regnant planets! Moralists malign presumptuous apostles by claiming they engage their souls with error at every turn. Ourselves, we draw no tangent.

More and more do we meet with Doctor Illuminatus who presumes to indulge every court from Aragon to Extremadura—debating and tossing the crust of matter while he likens earth's form to a melon. Granted. Yet he argues that should Spanish mines hold adequate mercury he might harvest the Mediterranean bed for ingenite gold! So goes he promenading through every court in Iberia save that of good sense. Discoursing much or little, how redoubtable we find the shifting face of Man.

We hear it alleged that from the jaws of some putrid corpse Philippus Theophrastus contrived to draw six gold particles which he judged must be the consequence of mineral virtue in that fragrant citizen—since how else could such wealth accumulate? Well, thaumaturgic considerations absorb our wit, causing us to shout and grow baffled and run through circles. Accordingly we suspect our Doctor misled himself. By turbith or unction do virulent diseases react against quicksilver whose essence gravitates to the mouth where it amalgamates with spittle, there to maturate unless it can be expelled—save that when a patient expires the essence will condense, moldering or festering throughout the carcass until purified and redeemed by liquefied atoms of degeneration after which it coagulates toward the likeness of gold. We have seen how by similar intent violets might spring from ashes, or stars that shine unequally must have their purpose, because nature resembles a chiming clock within which all subordinate wheels contribute their motion.

Behold the caudacity of man's estate! Pray for Theophrastus, disillusioned and sour, traveling home to his native village of Einsiedeln in the lofty canton of Appenzell, exchanging a troubled passage for eremetic contemplation. Ingratitude accompanied him and marked ascendencies while he wandered—yea! Poverty, neglect and ridicule trafficked at his heels like three mangy skulking mongrels. Therefore did he return bitterly to the ancient church that presided over his birth whose walls now loomed transparent, so much had he achieved with thirty-eight years. But in regard to that woeful journey we have heard enough, albeit little of what his parents were, which we think odd since precedents do not close where they began. Still, some say nobility lies more in the heart than birth. Concerning friends, we make out less, while of himself next to nothing. As for women, he kept no warm relationship, though of enemies a plenitude—thieves, derelicts and frauds, assassins, liars, buggers, cheats. And the wisdom of Avicenna he fed to the flames on a holiday, avowing that monumental rubbish merited its plume of smoke—to which we chant Amen!

At Salzburg expired our contradictory Philippus who was quack or psychikos—we know not which—in the Kaygasse, it is said, where he had engaged a chamber. He wrote how robbers at night creep in to steal if they cannot be seen, so creeps in cunning Death while medicine sits at its obscurity to steal away life, which is a man's greatest treasure. So the private way of God went to work to draw out his life, and we think he recognized that hand, giving directions for his burial at St. Sebastian's Church beyond the bridge. Bolstered half-upright on his couch he dictated to a local scribe how an erudite practitioner of medicine, Theophrastus von Hohenheim, being of clear mind committed life, death and soul to the care of an Almighty that would not permit the martyrdom and travail of His only Son to be fruitless, nugatory, one more sleeveless errand culled by a poor servant. Whereafter legacies were writ that all but paupers should forget. Two cartons of manuscripts and books he left at Augsburg, one at Kromau, various oddments at Leoben and in Carinthia—possibly at St. Veith or Villach. What a munificent estate! Some few burnished coins gibbering with loneliness, a patched cloak, boots, Concordia Bibliorum and Interpretationes super Evangelia badly frayed, ointments, knives, hostility sufficient for twelve plus the storage-vault of an insatiable mind. All work done—Lo, a misbegotten adept departed—this unlikely angel ascending from the Gasthaus zum Weissen Ross! Paradise is but a search for knowledge, he said, allotting his tormented years to that end and the public good. We doubt he had much choice. Disciples say the ferryman erred by thinking him three decades older, since as he knew so much more than cooks and servants Azrael mistook that countenance for one whose day was spent. But let it pass. In the hospital cemetery of Saint Sebastian we have examined a marble obelisk dedicated to Philippus Theophrastus, Alchymist and Physician, who with wondrous magic did cure the gout, leprosy and dropsy and bound up fearful wounds. There, by and large, he remains except his skull is gone—as though it could not quit travel. Just where this relic might be, who knows? We hear it exists in southern Bavaria and is thought to be that of some female. Yet we suspect a divine trumpeter draws winds together.

REGARDING the scrivener Flamel, we present our conspectus. That he dwelt in Paris near Saint Jacques-de-la-Boucherie in the notary street with his wife Perenelle is documented. And none save skeptics would dispute that on the seventeenth of January, Anno Domini 1382, he did successfully transmute eight ounces of mercury into an equivalent weight of silver, to which his wife stood witness—the assay exceeding proof. On the twenty-fifth of April, Perenelle again his deponent, our modest notary surpassed that achievement! O wonder upon wonder! We all but doubt our senses, we stagger from marvel to marvel. What next? Good Perenelle journeys to Switzerland, and Monsieur Flamel having interred in her vacant grave a Log respectfully publishes the date of her exit: Anno Domini 1399. But why? We confess bewilderment. Yea, we cudgel our brains. Where is the end to legerdemain? Lo, this artful scrivener—having distilled the Philosopher's Stone of limitless wealth and fountain of immortality—having buried on his own behalf another succedaneum, swiftly joins his devoted wife. Chymist Ninian Bres testifies that he saw them hundreds of years later on the Boulevard du Temple near the Opéra strolling arm-in-arm! Flamel, says he, was of moderate height, considerably bent by the passage of centuries but walked with a firm step and his eyes were lustrous. His skin looked translucent, not unlike alabaster. Concerning sweet Perenelle, she had somewhat aged. The two were attired in a style not long out of date, nonetheless a fustiness seemed to emanate from their clothes and as they came wandering toward a recess in the boulevard where Monsieur Bres waited, half-concealed beneath an arch—all sooty, reeking with sulphur, fingers discolored by acid—the Alchymist paused, gazing toward him as if about to speak, but cautious Perenelle drew her husband back into the crowd. Now we have seen on the fifth leaf of Figures d'Abraham Juif the face of an alchymist which we think must represent Flamel. If this be so, how do we refute the testament of Ninian Bres? We confess ourselves inadequate. But that a single musty clerk might touch the Stone seems to us implausible and undeserved, since if we do not surpass ourselves we have dropped asleep within a dream. Therefore, if mortal intent is gratification but nothing beyond, all has been accomplished. And therefore human intelligence has been wasted, although some turn to it while the gods claim yet another victim. And who would care how August winds prevail across Egypt? And who, like Thebet Benchorat, would assign four decades to find out the motions of an eighth sphere? Which among us would make miracles?

Very many earnest problems have been subjected to our thought: circumstantial conjuries, transformation, circular majesties, talismans riveted to amulets, redemption, trine and sextile aspects, magicians flush with snivel and windy smirks, bawds, panders, factors, malapert friars feeding on kickshaw,

flouts, taunts, counterfeit florins, crowns and angels, the mandrake voice sweeter than heavenly music—O, sediment in
abundance! And what becomes of charity? Accordingly we
look upon hermetic art with one eye shut because it is meant to
mislead travelers anticipating perfection. So let us contemplate
that miserable Puffer coughing, spewing up dark blood, full of
blasted hope, stuffed with fugitive rainbows, hail drumming the
glass while wife Meg yowls on his track for gold, exploring the
metallic souls of minerals caught in fuliginous envelopes with
obscurity the sign of his resolution, anticipating Erichthonius'
Basket, Deucalion's Coffer, the Tower of Danae—which is but
a Swamp of Lerna, less valuable than seaweed. Lybian quick-
sand drowns his entangled wit. Does he consult with Avicenna?
Does he ask if a thing is, then how is it? Or if it be not, how is it
not? Mayhap his skull was struck that same blow with which
many avow a Comet once struck the sun. See him crouch at the
furnaces of Borrichius, Beccher, Kunckel, Stahl—seeking one
rod of light. Now he computes the sand, now he counts the rain,
daubing and greasing, cloaked and wrapped with his hubris of
invincibility. What shall he whistle into a cage? See him peer
upon the shade of Gargoyles decorating mossy walls, consigned to measurements of electuary, bone-ash and orpiment
beneath some dusty bouquet of stale herbs that dangle from a
leaky roof—piss-guardian to pots of camphor and stibnite
jugs sweet as night-buckets, pasting together his porcelain
crock—this jack-leg porter to Bedlam logic. Listen to him
cough while he tabulates wages that would starve a cellar
mouse. Slop-slop! Drizzle-drizzle! Whistling stripes greet the
venturesome Adept, strangulation with a halter if his mouldy

metaphysic work-shop gives birth to that ineffable Regal Infant. Ague, cold soup, lice, cinders, mildewed bread—O yea! Apocalyptic images fade like tapestry. How long would our dove-tail chymist warm a splintered bench? Here does he squat—this ambitious novice in bleached velvet, alight to occult parallels. Observe him confront the universe by means of ichor, balm, gall, calx—Pelican plus White Cock plus the faithless Argent Vive. Now being told of some doctor that smeared yellow unguent over a peasant's fork to gild it our aspirant would do likewise. Thus every student replicates the art of his professor and struts in taverns like a deemster glutting his soul with lies. Therefore have we felt his pulse to speak of Gehazi—the impudent servant who turned covetous and opinionated after boasting accomplishments he had filched, unread, foppish, persuaded that he understood the Magnum Opus but got as his reward a Leprosie. So will others sicken upon rancid wine, puking, helpless, turgid with emrods, spite and livor, much like those storks which congregate on Asian plains where he that settles last is torn apart. Regard this Chymist. Watch him kneel by the hearth to pursue treasure, immortality and youth. Observe the tattered bundle vanish, old, emaciated, furious, grazing on bitter herbs yet devoted to uncertain art, unrepentant, dissolving among smoke and ashes. How handsomely does he illustrate affliction. Such a puddly life.

WE OURSELVES, have we not fled from imperfectly rubified metal and the odor of bauxite? We have essayed all—hair, blood and soul of Saturn, marcasites, aes astum, saffron of Mars, scales and dross of litharge, of iron, of antimony—all worth a rotted prune-pit. We have worked to extract oil and water from silver, calcined with salt or without salt, yet our best efforts failed. We derive no advantage. Toward antique grandeur have we labored, assisted by ardent and corrosive liquid. By recourse to vitriol and salammoniac with egg-shell orpiment have we sought the Stone which achieves consummation through putrefaction. The Green Lion did not help. Saffron of Mars proved inefficacious. Celandines, secundines, rennet, salt attincar, salt alembrot, none disclosed its secret. Nor would the sperm of falling stars—sophic brass! So we have pummeled froth! We have heard quaint music! Mercuric ointments have we congealed and mixed into triumphant minerals, thinking thereby to succeed—joining those that struggle toward multiplication and amalgamation. With constancy and perseverance have we multiplied one-third of nothing. Not simple albifaction but rubifaction have we witnessed—receipts with congelations, sophistications from Navarre to Germany. Lo! All proved Limbus, the wily cube of nature escaped. Now here and there did we meet one or two claiming to know another who possessed that Formula, yet never could we make his acquaintance. So is it not familiar? Is it not a lugubrious concert?

AGAINST the Incertus with every vain science were we advised by Cornelius Agrippa—those that constitute medicine, physic or metaphysic, dialectic, geometry, arithmetic, music, poetry, cosmography and jurisprudence, pious superstition, principles, alchymy and the craft of memory. He does bloat with eloquence does our tutor, he thickens with those divulgations of wisdom which map out solitary minds. And how shall he address himself to the mermaid's shoulder when midnight turns?

Some Flanders chymist pretends that by a stranger's generosity he was granted a morsel of the essence we seek, which sparkled like powdered glass and upon which he projected half-a-pound of quick-silver—this mineral congealing toward yellow slag with excellent virtue that weighed almost as much. Therefore he chose to believe in the truth of alchymic magistery, albeit he could not by any method analyze the constituents of his gift nor saw his benefactor again. O mercy! So did Virgil, Horace, Ovid and Vitruvius call this elusive substance their tenement. Democritus fabricated jewels at Memphis while Cneius Pompeius Magnus returned triumphantly to Rome from Syria with an optic Lens through which he descried multitudes of distant soldiers! Miracle succeeds miracle. Ah, but we suspect we testify enough against putative testament, more than enough to question each supposed triumph, hazarding that metamorphosis resemble the Friar's Lantern—ignis fatuus—a migrant globe.

What marks the scope or ambit of any man? How shall we divide the interior of divergent spheres? Do we not gauge the wind without knowing what hurls from its belly? Meister John Picus de Mirandola writes in De Auro how concerning gold and silver he saw these confected on sixty occasions, and of a reputable chymist that he twice had pulled out gold from pig-iron. Well, we are indebted to John Picus for nine hundred splendid theses pertaining to logic, divinity, mathematics, Kabbalism and kinetics. Indeed we feel obligated, yet narrow enquiries administer our thought. Have we not studied seventeen volumes on venesection by that occasional doctor of Padua, Horatius Augenius? Meanwhile we count nine hundred duplicities issuing from a white palace that like medlars rot in the mid-day sun. O yea, we do squint. We listen and look asquint.

No EVIDENCE of duality have we detected in twenty-one volumes incorporating the opera omnia of Albert de Groot, nor traces of black art. No more did he preach sorcery than make pistols or cannon, which inventions have been charged against him by Matthias de Luna. But that he did value some curious element branded with the image of a serpent provided by Dominicans, and that reptiles came slithering to visit this counterpart—so much is true. Still, the degrees of a circle which chart our circumference sub-serve magisteries within.

Now since Bath Abbey was dismantled, laborers have unearthed out of an ancient niche or cranny—we know not just where—a glass filled with noxious tincture which was thrown aside onto a dunghill. And the vile heap forthwith turned scarlet, so for many years the corn grew up in Bathwicke field marvelous green and rank and abundant, as this was testified by old men that could recall, and agreed with by a cobbler that saw it—yclept Foster or Belcher. But very much news comes singing with the wind. Clouds sail on to Denmark.

We WONDER how extravagance stops if men rush to vouch-safe extravagant tales. We have heard of Saint Germain's father that he was a salamander and his mother a Muslim princess, and he thought it no great feat to draw spots from diamonds. Anon, we grow persuaded that he traded both eyes for hooks and beneath the roof of his friend, Prince of Hesse Cassel, this Quacksalver expired to the winding from a strange horn one overcast night at Sleswig—and doubt not that at the bar he lifted up both hands to plead innocent! Yet as the rabbit senses no limit to timidity nor the ferret to killing because one was born timid, the other murderous, so each has a claim and temperament but did not invent his traits. Nor can a man invent himself, thus it becomes comic to argue that he behave other than he did, being born of ramous and globulous parts—his head standing still while his brains pirouette.

O LISTEN listen! Pouring juice of fennel together in a glass with a buck goat's blood diluted by vinegar—should any man dare to anoint his face with this panpharmacon he will utter dreadful and audacious things. Or should the blood of Cyboi, which the Greeks call Iphim, be emptied into a lizard's skin and a man drink it—Behold! Some will say he stands like a giant with his face lost among stars. And this possibility we admit, but we consider also how very often men's eyes are shut tight like those of birds asleep from November to January.

AIBATHEST. Alborach. Serinech. Zibach. What? What? Fugitive Serf. Glass of Pharaoh. Immaculate Lamb. What does it mean? Numus. Ethelia. Thabitris. Corsufle. Boritis. Mercy!

Mercy! Artephius tells us that from the soul of the body Whiteness arises. Morien assures us that the second operation is but a repetition of the first. Matter being fixed in the bottom of the vase, says d'Espagnet, Jupiter puts Saturn to flight and takes possession of the kingdom to assume its government. Splendid! We smite our brow with admiration. Redness we find to be a continuation of the decoction of matter. Imbibition we learn is a time when condensing vapors descend upon sophic earth in the bottom of the vessel. Truly do we feel informed, as though we had spent the hour listening to hags, Egyptians and such-like, as each expounds what gives him satisfaction. Is there not more concord among snakes? Six metals at first we represent as bare-headed Slaves kneeling before the King, but after transmutation they wear a Crown! So do they propose to explain enigmas with enigmas. And were we handed a platter why should we not catch the Moon?

Spring seems a time inordinately pleasant to the bee, which likes to spend his hours collecting honey or wax. Pillage and rape are gratifying activities to the wolf, which lusts after the delicate flesh of ewes and lambs. Rivers appear wondrously agreeable to loitering fishes idly basking and swaying in the current of their element. But what seems pleasurable to Man? Furious, dissatisfied from birth he staggers out to gaze at he knows not what, then off he flies into all countries possessed of stories and tales spun by his cataract of thought. Praise God, we think men celebrate their passage in wise foolishness, dancing goats embossed on silver cups.

JOHN, Abbot of Westminster, much devoted to untrustworthy authors scattering falsehoods that lead toward whirlpools of misrepresentation, forfeited thirty years of his life in vain attempts to father the Regal Child. Cannot any man be subject to error? Aye, but fools persist. So we conclude this world was tossed on a blanket. So is the alchymist wise to sublimate desire like an elderly virgin in her quiet room pinning butterfly wings to a painted board.

NOW let us render homage to Magister Bernard de Trévisane misapprehending gold for mercury coagulated by the resolve and inimitable strength of sulfur. Look upon his magistery! Haply assisted by that monk from Citeaux, yclept Geofroi de Lemorier, this ambitious pharmacist vowed he would separate the yolks from the whites of two thousand chicken eggs. Yea! What next? He would mortify in dung this auspicious yellow residue, from which he meant to distil or congeal a panacea. We think aspirants that choose a foot-path among labyrinths of apparent contradiction, cautiously eschewing predilection or lumpish misconjecture, will anoint themselves with glory. Not so our misguided innocent subordinating life and wealth and holy reputation to one egregious sophistry. O, how often do we hear men debate across the sun, comprehending too much or too little.

FRESH talk of a great English Philosopher or Mathematic— we know not which—that spends each afternoon inspecting bubbles puffed out of his clay pipe, and all bemused with attractive color believes chymists of Schemnitrium have conspired to liberate noble copper from gross iron! Woe is us! Might we contend that Egypt's monarch Hermes compounded an universal solvent? Did he not? Incredulity being as hurtful as credulity, we would essay all matter while holding tight to what has been ordained, mistaking not ormolu for royal metal. That presumptuous shards of ice after centuries underground might accomplish their destiny by changing to rock crystal, as many believe, we ourselves would no more certify than dispute—elements being subject within themselves neither to change nor growth, unalterable and incontrovertible, one after the next. Yet the integrity of this universe has been dictated by homogeneous aspects. Therefore nature's purpose must be to establish and fix the highest above the lowest, despite resident impurities, winding up Scripture in a nut-shell.

We have heard of some Italian who pontificates upon our world—that it is encompassed by others, all twisting through space, and argues for moving particles, saying Heat is a mere swarm of corpuscles and Heaven might be solid! We suspect Jesuits will fry his flesh for the motions of his mouth. As children we are ignorant, says he, but being conscious of deficiencies we admit to ignorance. Yet as we are brought up to the habit of discipline in our house we listen to the faith and custom and rituals and conduct of our adversaries being subject to vilification since these do not sound orthodox, much as they have been instructed about us with the temper of our affairs. And within us are scattered a multitude of improvident forces so that in others various customs will beat down their paths, and therefore it is axiomatic that what impedes our progress must be meant for humiliation and slaughter—which we accept as agreeable and tributary since antagonists in their conceit do the like, and pledge obeisance to what deities they worship for having vouchsafed the light of immortality upon assurances equaling our own. Now all this does he preach, but all in vain since new divinity follows new philosophy. Let him consider the firmament from the Campo de' Fiori with his logic, limited as we must be to a universe where delicate arguments postulate others more misleading and difficult. Yet we stand astonished before the passion of his intellect—which some label a Sword that needs close handling. Skeptics and fanatics we must admit make good brothers.

Dame Nature adopts strange children. Look upon Petrus d'Abano questioned in his eightieth year by suspicious ecclesiarchs. That Petrus did immerse or replenish his soul with oracular science, that he could summon spent coins back to his pocket and did hold hostage within a Crystal wicked spirits— so much was alleged. And being adjudged guilty by reason of circuitous answers our aged recusant expired before his auto-da-fé! Is not Satan a master of versatility? Thus at Padua, close by the village of his birth, was a likeness in straw substituted for our departed apostate and set afire. Ah well, we suspect pointed shoes fit the fisherman no better than mortar boards balance the brains of zealots.

Pope John XXII having ascended to heaven by way of Avignon, Anno Domini 1334, we think his estate might be worth mention. We count eighteen million Florins with jewelry to the value of seven, plus innumerable consecrated goblets he acquired through hermetic craft, since we know this worldly pontiff each night submitted to anagogic indoctrination from Brother Arnold, meanwhile interdicting divinatory art. Distribution of transfigured bread and wine, a magic laying-on of hands—by such shameless investiture does Christian ceremony proclaim its merit. Who can measure humanity's divagation?

Praise we hear for the shrewdness of a British ecclesiastic that purchased a flourishing brothel with sacerdotal funds. And is he subject to blame? We know how men in their hearts hide one thing while from their mouths comes another. Do we therefore extend as a terror to malfeasance the reprobation of posterity? Did not Jehovah pour the truth into blemished vessels? Aye, he did. Besides, such unscrupulous enterprise seems much less apt to fail than prosper, and on this logic we observe salvation recede from us, not we from it.

Well, we have watched men flying toward fulfillment like bees frantic for honey. We have watched others crouch like spiders taut with poison. Some attribute sibylline power to the mole—at which Pliny scoffs—while others would eat the palpitating heart of a weasel. So do men pour liquids up and down, or one into this, another into that, all brewing mixtures from sunrise onward. Avicenna teaches that where any matter rests upon salt it becomes salt and what stands on a stinking place will stink. Natures move indissolubly toward their own.

Now we have heard men offering contraries as principles until Proteus himself could not differ so much. Still, did this not hold true for Hippocrates? And we ourselves submit to deeper discrepancies and quarrels within than ever we met on the cobbled streets of Ingolstadt. Divers indeed is the mind's apparel! How queer. Fustian sleeves, tattered lining. See us step forth adorned with intricate riddles and figures. But have lines fallen down about us at pleasant places? Do we feel pinched with straightness?

Are men less apt to lose their reason than be lost to it? Let us contemplate the labor of Meister Alexander Sethon with his difficult progress toward a coagulation of gold, fluttering from province to province across the Continent, squawking like a rooster that would escape its monarch's table, stripped of amity and denied the magisterial fruit, imprisoned by Christian, Elector of Saxony, for refusing to express the Inexpressible—until the bloody wreckage of our recalcitrant chymist was rewarded with molten lead. Such a spectacle! Does iniquity adhere to suffering flesh? Could it be true of God that He lives with careless ease? Being totally good, does He love none but Himself?

What of Thomas Aquinas objecting that every yellow mineral must qualify as gold? How is this? We listen to him declare in Thesaurus Alchymiae how the purpose of mystic experiment should be transference of metals from imperfect to perfect, avowing that he believes in such a possibility! O, paradox upon paradox! Next, in tractates addressed to Frater Regnauld he discourses upon his search for an essence to tinge mercury that would pierce any known substance while overcoming fire! Under which meridian do we live?

𝔑ᴇxᴛ, of Roger Bacon we hear that he would study the furious multiplicities of light while simultaneously projecting gold through revelation of natural ligatures. We suspect Providence does award small things to the small, so do large minds reach out toward nimble motions, fortified against divisible shapes like scattered mercury seeking to collect and reunite itself. Is not a man's thought marvelous at its operation?

𝔓ɪᴇᴛɪsᴛs look to colonies of God. Others go walking in Corsica. Jakob Böhme fixedly gazing toward the burnished pewter dish embarks upon his celebrated trance during which he remarks Chaos transfigured. Ah, the watchful dog! Grant him a papal throne and the triune mitre! Yet we do not forget Valentinus observing how vision disappears if gnomic art disintegrates. Should we like Nestorians slice apart the nature of Jehovah to put aboard some Narrenschiff where black winds draw?

𝔉ᴏᴜʀ passions like the wheels of a carriage transport us from one estate to the next—which are called Joy, Love, Desire and Hate—as the moon and sun are said to pirouette and whirl across our semesters while encircling the earth—or as three superior planets dance about, now stationary, now direct, being now retrograde or in apogee or perigee, slow, swift, oriental or occidental, gracefully undulant—or as Mercury with Venus

trails harping about the universe and four phantasmic lights
wink toward Jupiter, all belike to handsome music out of the
spheres. Hence few stand amazed to see men sport the frenzied
look of squeezed cats.

𝔚ITH what anxiety do we discard one object for its neighbor
while juggling tumultuous ideas of what we want, delirious,
everywhere presuming the utmost gratification, so accustomed
are we to seek benefits where we believe they should be met. We
listen to Frater Albertus propose that men renounce home,
take leave of bewildered families, debase honorable lineage and
pitch fortune to the sea while enduring disease, hunger and
thirst in order to scour tropic latitudes—but for what? That
they might search out fugitive chimeras faintly descried in a
wordless dream! Now what are these? Longevity, liberty and
gold. O, such a tongue for such a tiny monk of tiny wit! Yet are
we told that he despaired of what his habit demanded until the
gracious Virgin vouchsafed excellence at Divinity or Philosophy whereupon he most imprudently chose the second, for
which she chastised him since as he stood to the rostrum lecturing at the university in Cologne and all his thoughts thickly
encrusted with jewels of rhetoric—Woe! Every idea fled! Yea,
he fell mute. Therefore, if we reflect upon Frater Albertus we
avow that having been transmogrified from an ass to a philosopher he was converted back again. Mercy! What fearful trag-
edies ambush the scholiast! We feel stricken. We sigh with re-
morse. We think mortals exhibit greater brains in their heels
than up above.

Ho! Comes this most respected monk journeying from Bollstaedt wagging his plump book lately printed at Nuremberg—Compendium theologicae veritatis—which excited pedagogues. What a splash do these mighty buckets make! Withal we find wisdom difficult to communicate since rung aloud it gives off the uncommon ring and chime of common folly. We ourselves like spinning spiders wisely restrict our wisdom to its net.

Well, what do we say about Asses? We listen to Frater Cornelius Agrippa assert with his Vanity of Sciences how it is prudent to be transported on the back of one—the beast exemplifying both patience and fortitude. And in regard to that of Balaam, we consider it more discerning and perceptive than its master since it learnt to speak intelligibly. And of the philosopher Ammonius—each day he allowed an ass to audit his lecture. We know also how Abraham chose to take his seat upon an ass. And Jesus Christ, so did he recognize the incomparable merit of this lowly creature by selecting an ass for the occasion of his terrestrial entrance. Therefore, it seems to us that few animals are so appropriate to honor and to uphold Man's irrefutable superiority.

Magister Vaughan in Coelum Terrae reflects on the mephitic Dragon which is everywhere present, out of whose nostrils stems a loathsome fire that presages imminent destruction, and with touching modesty labels himself the Egg of Nature. Pious he is. Indeed he drips effacement, conceived by God while admitting to weakness, equivalent to father and mother, invisible, visible, within the light is he as well as without, signifying both heaven and earth. Simultaneously is he bright or dark, sprung from the soil while descending toward mankind from above, disseminating every color, a carbuncle of the Sun transmuting copper, iron, lead and other subordinate minerals into predestined shapes. What? So did we read with Fulcanelli how innumerable secrets have been carved into the Great Porch of Notre Dame—which edifice patiently outlasts the centuries in silence while it awaits one adept capable of understanding. Bravo! To every sort of incantation we cry Alleluia!

EIRENAEUS explains how a furious cur upon a snarling bitch will generate a pallid whelp the color of wisdom. Indeed! Further, he informs us how two embattled dogs—one Armenian, one Corascene—illustrate this principle more tenaciously than opposing magnets contend, or as jousting knights reveal how combat opening with violence must end with coalescence. Seldom have we felt more enlightened. Now off to the alembic for there in a glass haply we may watch earth turn to water and water turn to air and air to flame and then down again, meanwhile between each working many things worth admiration. But how many horses shall we requisition to transport such masterful conceit?

TAGLA! Mathon! Johovam! Eloim! Five measures of sulfur, of saltpeter seven, of hazel twigs three. Nature's time be long, the manner of her concoction uniform. Her fire appoints our need, therefore be Gold the precious plasm. Gold be insurgent!

This is helpful—wrapped in frantic or obfuscous effort—yet what do such mutterings propose? We could as readily drown flies beneath a squirt of water as interpret mystic twattle, and we inquire as skeptics what is not boxed up with fraud? Is it best to frolic in obscurantries of expression or in expressions of obscurity? Ambiguities, wool, smoky promise. Our wits do grow stuck at one place like the dried-out bristles of last year's varnish brush. Where does such gibberish end? The nucleus of spagyric mystery is life and the glorious key there-to is Light, whose gleaming ore the alchymist exposes. What? What? Back and forth we swim, captive trout in a barrel. From this we should borrow a magnet, or chalybs from that, Diana's Doves from elsewhere—flats and sharps to promote confusion. Mayhap we have drifted off to sleep in Hilary's cradle at Poictiers whence so many travel full of prayer and ceremony and bring stunned relatives, where lunatics bed down to retrieve their brains.

WE HEAR of peasants annually gathering upon their pilgrimage to weep outside some Bavarian chapel where six centuries past a flask of our physic Red Lion spilled and discolored the soil, so now they lift up their hands to praise what they consider miraculous. So does that reliquary holding four knuckle-bones of Ramon Lull work miracles at Mallorca while colleges founded across the continent dedicate their curricula to Ars Lulliana. And our world stands motionless since that is what the Church has taught, therefore earthquakes do not exist and tremors we experience are merely the consequence of febrile imagining. Bravo! Bravo! Let us silence the voice of commotion.

Circles widen. Friar Bacon would convince us how this world might be circumnavigated. Aye, perhaps. Contentious scholars disagree. Yet all swear he lends the devil his brain to whet, for which he deserves excommunication. Aye, perhaps. Even so he would separate common usage from theoretical understanding, and since there is much advantage to the former he thinks it superior—which many have called the trade-mark of a plebian mind. Ourselves, we find these indivisible. Sooner or later every man is caught among oppositions like a turtle in a net and overturned, stripped of hope. But we have studied deeper in his important book, Frater Rogerius Baco de Secretis Artis & Naturae, that privately was brought out by the Franciscan to discuss unnatural perfections of lightning and thunder—since by themselves nitre and sulfur and charcoal contribute nothing, whereas mingled they yield to command a monstrous foaming crack and most black foul stink. O, thoroughly foul! And he proposes to rarefy the atmosphere through vile flame which he expects to ignite with phosphorus! Or contrive an aeronautic chariot lofting passengers to and fro—out of this or that province! Or construct a Pump to inhibit and control the wind through pressures! In truth, our cunning friar waxes fat on speculation nourished by celibate dreams while drawing angles above triangles, mistaking intellect for soul.

𝕹OTHING about nature may be incredible but we observe her. Now we could dwell upon Double Nativity and first or second sublimation, visible or invisible, without which no essence could be extracted from its animus. We might discourse upon sulfurs compounded or elementary, or three-fold Argent Vives and thrice as many cathartics. O yea! Now what of this Lion rampant in his mangy carcase? Or what of Christian sacrament? Ourobouros, that wily viper professing neither commencement nor end, devours his tail while we have consumed six decades questioning verities.

𝕷o! COMES an uninvited minstrel with a dirty cape and a boil suppurating on his nose criss-crossed beneath furious scars, one eye shut against us—some ancient soldier! Ripe enough, rank to be near, singing about savage divorce while the gods retreat and wicked angels comport, urging the world downward to impenitent violence, brigandage, plunder, when terrestrial equilibrium will be sacrificed, sailors be loath to navigate far from shore, Heaven lack for starlight and planets deviate, swerving out of their true direction, when earth's atmosphere does not replenish itself, when fertile soil sinks to velleity leaving turgid fruits to rot unripe with venom. And from this much will come down faster than lightning even as men cry out too late in useless tongues—delivering their dream too late. Such a bundle of curiosities.

𝕽umors of a wandering magus conceived in heresy and mistrust . . .

𝕴T MAY not be within us to want or love what is foreign. Oriental alchymists teach that the body resembles a state with the diaphragm comparable to a palace, legs and arms to boundaries or suburbs, bones and joints to officials, blood to ministers, breath to the populace. But I wonder. Also, it is said they prescribe an elixir of potable gold, claiming this will suffuse interior organs to insulate us against mortal requirements because gold does neither rot nor melt although subject to lengthy burial with extensive calefaction. And I have heard they speak of one anointed except for the soles of his feet with the Grand Catholicon which inhibits decay, who would not walk but rode softly, expecting by this deception to swindle fate. Nevertheless he fell sick, dying from corruption after nine centuries. It seems improvident to denounce or mock unfamiliarities, but the heart and mind give contrary counsel.

$\mathfrak{A}$VICENNA asserts that imagination exercises fearful power, sufficient to make a camel fall down groaning. I disagree while admitting that imagination is very strong, necessary to digest sensual perceptions. The fixed and jeweled stare of a toad I know to be fatal. That nubile witches enfeeble amorous men by some lascivious concentration of their gaze I do not doubt. And in Tibet the focus of thought produces demons called Egrigors. Then, too, I have observed whelps swimming upon the urine of patients afflicted with rabies—which could be simulacra swimming through iniquitous logic. How such matters precipitate in the brain I cannot be sure. I suspect that imagination might resemble a kind of Warmth or a fluctuous Light given to nervous anxiety.

$\mathfrak{I}$ DOUBT if the course of an injury derives from magnitude so much as the circumstances of acquisition. Under Gemini or Virgo or Capricorn very few prognoses can be favorable. Similarly, wounds contracted past noon are less auspicious than matinal injuries. But the intent of sidereal influence baffles us. By what principle does moonlight draw interior fluids outward, yet stimulate a salubrious warming within? Often the physician is reduced to wonder.

$\mathfrak{W}$HETHER night-fall should be traced to a declining sun or to the ascendant stars of night I am unable to say, nor if occasional planets could be shaped like cucurbits, nor if aboriginal populations have descended from Adam, nor if Eve acquired her genitals by drinking snow-water after the fall from grace—as those people of Carinthia are thought to acquire goiter—nor if living underground there be divers imperceptible creatures such as melusines, nymphs, sirens, lorinds, gnomes. But that we were given rudimentary senses in order to apprehend and thus direct our future, I have little doubt. Still, we seem compacted or locked into a kind of petrification. Human existence oddly replicates the life of stone, which I find curious. Regardless of how much knowledge a physician accumulates he will be surprised by anomalies—such as a white raven—which confute all of his books and all of his experience and what he has discovered at the sick-bed.

I THINK each component of each organism enjoys its life, being succeeded by its death, so we meet resurgent orders of death and resurrection prosecuting life. Consequently everything interior that has conducted itself privately will emerge after deterioration to reveal a countenance. Thus, should some infant's life conclude after five hours we surmise those bodily planets have made their circuit. Hence, the alchymic doctor looks to organic interactions, each having a predestined end and commencement.

EXTRINSIC and intrinsic worlds surely must correspond. Liver, brain, heart, lungs, spleen, bowels and kidneys—all of this implies concord between planets and organs. Hildegard teaches that every matter has been so devised upon exceeding grace that none consents to separation, each will surrender its being, each will quit or cease if prevented by force from mutual association.

I MARVEL at the vigilance with which nature coordinates dissimilar entities. Why does she situate the lungs near the heart? For refreshment? No. A more important office of these indefatigable bellows is to inhale and to convey to the heart an ethereal spirit. So if we feel agitated we breathe with great passion because of spiritual waste which nature is attempting to restore.

No SENTIENT creature has been denied a capacity for thought. In the case of animals, we observe their various affections and season of mating, the nourishment and care and defense of their young, their expressions of goodwill or hostility toward human masters, and so forth. All this being evident, it follows that the souls of animals must have been endowed with the ability to reason or with a propensity to meditate, but as this seems restricted to their appetites and desires they do not reflect upon the world's renovation.

VEGETABLES display mental faculties, however subordinate to those of humans, animals and minerals. They reproduce and augment themselves, they perceive changes of weather, they observe and conform to every season, they germinate at the appropriate hour—burying their roots, extending and developing their leaves—proving that they understand and foresee. If a vegetable has been planted in poor soil adjacent to rich soil, why does it lean toward the latter? How does it know? If the female and male are planted apart what directs their inclination?

Great sympathies must exist to bring about the preservation of this terraqueous globe. Or like a foolish dog do I elect to bark at shadows?

Let us assume the refulgence of Venus were extinguished, then what attraction should persuade minerals or animals or vegetables or humans to proliferate? I cannot be sure, but men collect knowledge as they pluck fruit from trees, and since we do not deny our counsel overhead it follows that doctors should study the rise of pre-eminent planets if they would resolve uncertainties below.

It appears that celestial embodiments of both sexes converse with each lavishing ideas upon its opposite, so that either will endorse a lascivious invitation. Hence they are subject to conspiracy, plotting together, albeit the forms of women seem more flammable.

As to how feminine lust contrives to preside over masculine—this is because a fluid element requires a blazing element, which accounts for the wife who succumbs to internal craving while the husband is apt to become obstinate or contentious, suspicious and bewildered by her passion. Latent difficulties belabor him. Still he feels lost without his wife, since then he is but a peripatetic disembodied shade—an anguished voice striving to incorporate itself, because once she was the rib and crooked piece of him. Had she otherwise been created than from his body, how was concupiscence bequeathed to them both? We are told by Saint Augustine of the lamp dedicated to Venus which could not be extinguished, implying that blood and flesh have nothing to impart but relentless desire.

𝕹EITHER the masculine nor the feminine demands intercourse, merely its essential nature. Why should providence create but half a soul? Or how should Adam feel reconciled to Eve unless she arose within his heart? The woman to whom a man binds himself through intimate congress with declarations of fidelity becomes a part of him, nor can he divorce her by ceremonious pretext or separation, their constituence being one. Nor is it bone or flesh pledging to construct secret attachments so much as carnal intelligence. Even so she remains his best friend, his redeemer—for having lost the key to heaven, unconscious of that light extant in him before he went to sleep in spirit and wakened in the flesh, he would stoop down and lower himself to lower degradation if she did not stand on the threshold offering in exchange for that neglected refuge a vision of terrestrial paradise radiant with the promise of unification.

𝕴 SUSPECT men are driven to seduce women by an impatience which is enlarged because of their counterpart's proximity, or by speculation or by contact, as a splinter of dry wood ignites when exposed to the burning overtures of sunlight. Men become absorbed by visceral tendencies to reflection, hence passion inexorably mounts, which is the first cause of masculine fluid accumulating. Within the female corpus expedients further their own resolve much as the lodestone draws mineral by an inward-sucking of private necessity.

𝕿RIPLETS and greater multiples occur if the frantic womb contracts with more than a single breath while gathering semen for itself. Should it accept the liquid of animals a mooncalf will be born, such is uterine strength.

𝕸ENSTRUAL blood that commixes with male sperm subjected to putrefaction creates the basilisk, which is poisonous and fatal, although this monstrosity does not live long, being recruited by Satan. Yet for what purpose? Alchymic physicians grope and stumble through swirling mist.

𝖂HENCE comes the Spanish disease? I attribute it to writhing succubi begot in brothels as a result of useless fornication. Although I believe this to be the cause, I admit uncertainty. Like the pseudo-medicus do I shift and feint and make systems so that one might think God consulted me to draw up His world out of my nothingness. As for parasites, I think these develop whenever male and female bodies are committed to lewd espousal. But how are they brought? By equatorial wind?

𝕯ISCREPANCIES such as hare-lip, scabrous nerves and acephali might be a consequence of female imagining perhaps engendered by insufficient phlogiston resulting from befoulment of vapors in the evolutionary matrix. How often I meet outlines or accumulations of female thought, yet do they seem my own. What doublet is this?

𝕾HOULD feminine imagery predominate during generative congress the woman will deliver a boy. Hence, the opposite must be true. But suppose that the pregnant woman, while clutching her knee, should think about a snail—then would the knee of this infant reproduce its mother's thought? Yes. But why? In Pietra Santa lived a very devout woman who knelt to pray beneath a picture of John the Baptist, subsequently being delivered of a child with luxuriant hair and a long beard. As the seedling aspires to that firmament whence fell its procreative seed, all things necessarily return to the source of their inspiration.

Monthly female blood emboldens something diabolic in the heart whence it radiates but periodically returns, evaporating when subject to distillation. This is how sensual influences escape, expanding and contracting and darkening the aether, suborning the minds of men drawn down to these sour planetary exhalations of women—humidium menstrui. The odious red toad which dwells among brambles engenders astonishment when he bloats with magic, but his sorcery fails to equal that of this fluid which corrodes iron, mottles the looking-glass, blemishes the glow of polished ivory, turns linen black, empties bee-hives, blights green fruit and spoils the edge of razors, driving domestic creatures insane, sucking vitality from blossoms. I suspect it may be as perilous as that sealed image or concept of hatred which the toad, born with some natural aversion to humanity, nourishes in his brain, equivalent to the breath of a hag. Maria Prophetissa has taught the admixture of Man—pale semen, menstrual blood—luminescence brought to a Stone in the dark. Aye, this is possible.

MUCH remains to be learned, but I think it has been documented in cases from Zurich to Madrid that the odorous under-garments of females during their period become saturated with excitement. Also, with the help of this noxious effluent wives are enabled to excel their husbands at wicked contrivance. So much appears indisputable, yet I recognize contingencies. Exposing falsehood is easier than disclosing truth.

WITHOUT question the minds of women anticipate endless journeys to kingdoms that men fail to descry. Yet toward what prospect? It is well known how during sleep they depart from their bodies in order to congregate on flowering meadows where they revisit and review the incontinent past by means of lubricious conceit, and I think many so employ or distract themselves while awake. What could be the nervous root of this? I admit I do not know, but satisfaction resulting from imagination encourages anxiety, hence I advise oestrual patients to avoid salacious dreams and shadowy apartments. I consider it possible that during sabbatic levitation some employ belladonna, seated astride foxes, goats, swine, bears, weasels, donkeys, or such-like lickerish animals which ravenously escort them through low-scudding moist clouds rocking and howling with sensuous delight from Le Puys-de-dôme and Mount Paterno and the Horselberg slope as far as Portugal or the island of Crete. Whispering and muttering and inventing voluptuous gestures, they descend at midnight to model spirits on their own. As to why they do this, the cause may be Lucifer who understood that for mankind to grow rebellious and carnal and independent the sexes should be separate. Thus he sculpted and displayed to the eyes of mortal men his vision of a future, so that they became filled with enthusiasm and lusted for women who promised pleasures hitherto unimagined. Then with eagerness they grouped themselves about the Rebel—superseding the intent of Jehovah.

THAT concupiscent women welcome fiendish embraces culminating in diabolic intercourse I think undeniable. Without contrition some admit guilt, others elect to remain silent as the cuckold goes about his business. We have heard how Elizabeth the Queen on her deathbed lay ringed with fire—for what I do not guess, although I suspect that the bodies of women majestic to behold contain dark and turbid entrails.

WE OBSERVE how in the celebrated case of Walpurga Hausemännin she misled a susceptible bondsman, Schlumpberger, by devious argument until he participated in unholy congress. Having been reduced by query and torture, she disclosed that she copulated not with this man but the Devil himself—wearing his raiment—who privately had scratched his ensign upon her left shoulder, who inquired if she would mortgage her soul and with a quill guided her hand to the contract which she subscribed in blood. Further, she confessed to riding at night before this escort, straddling a pitchfork, and adored this Black Prince to whom she knelt and to whom she prayed, who slapped her in the face because she spoke the name of Jesus—whom she at once cursed and disavowed in order to be baptized afresh, renamed Höfelin. She admitted to rubbing her genitals with salve out of a box, of causing the death of four cows and various pigs and geese, and on Saint Leonard's Day had exhumed the corpse of a child which she then devoured, collecting the hair and gnawed bones for witchcraft to sweep hail across a field at Siechenhausen. Also, she brought up frost beside the low gate at the garden of Peter Schmidt during some witches' revel. And were it not for intervention by the Almighty she would have damaged more. So much being alleged, Herr Marquard, Bishop of Augsburg and Provost of the Cathedral, calling upon imperial prerogative, delivered to this sorceress a sentence of death by immolation and by Common Law remanded all of her goods to the Treasury. Bound and seated backward on a cart she was then transported to the place of execution where her right hand was amputated and her naked body subjected numerous times to a glowing iron. So that nothing about her would be visible above the earth or below, her ashes were emptied into the nearest flowing water. Thus was the manifesto of God corrupted. Punishment prevailed because it is understood how justice depends upon retaliation. Now, it appears plain that constellations mount toward heaven as opposites decline, this being paramount to the world. Still I wonder if the cause of lewd unconformity might be fuliginous aether emanating from a damaged skull, since what is exterior might affect what is interior. These influences I suspect are reciprocal, therefore subject to misfunction. Like the juggler an astute physician must toss or balance various concepts.

THERE is reason to suppose that devils inhabit our provinces as comfortably as they inhabit the ocean depths, crepuscular forests, precipices or deserts. They have been seen gathering for the sabbat in Westphalia and Thuringia and at the Spirato della Mirandola in Italy and in the Carpathians on the Babia Gora, streaming thence and elsewhere out of their apartments in earth's inaccessible pockets with little regard to distance. Pliny avows that he saw with his own eyes the birth of cinnabar from the blood shed on sandy soil by an elephant and a dragon locked in mortal combat—which many dispute. But facts do not cease to exist by virtue of being ignored, and I have observed demons fornicate not only upon each other but with complaisant humans, which admixture produces cambions. Is nature to blame for divergencies? I do not know.

$\mathcal{I}$ HAVE seen how the demon of lust Osmodeus seizes possession of aching bodies for an instant of carnal enjoyment. Later, with passion assuaged, he discards this abused and mutilated flesh. And because I have seen our proclivity to rummage for wealth amid putrescence, I wonder if we may seek resurrection atop a dung-heap. But that is theology's hospice.

$\mathcal{V}$ENAL malaise or bewitchment—how might it be cured? Noisome vapors from smouldering waste compel the animus to withdraw, alleviating symptoms because phlogiston lapidifies the brain. Still, such counteractives may prove useless due to opacities that frequently develop among women of exquisite temperament, some of whom will contrive to poison the aliment they prepare for their husbands, being drugged or stupefied with licentious imagery. Women of this type should be dissuaded from suckling and from playing with receptive children because of debauched or meditative coercions. I do not know how women so possessed are to be helped. They seem to know more than I—deceitfully pretending to ask advice. I would grasp the blind root of a universe were I able to address such darkness.

$\mathfrak{H}$ow is the salacious female to be considered? I am uncertain because I think the status of woman honorable and significant insofar as she is man's instrument of pleasure, experienced at oestrus, mistress of the night, ripe with magic property, more passionate than the dawn. Yet she is an uncontrollable ungovernable wind tumbling down a hill. She is like the tree bearing fruit, and man is like the fruit she has borne. If we consider what injuries the tree can sustain but how much less its fruit, by so much is she superior.

$\mathfrak{T}$HAT women grow lascivious and preoccupied with venery after marriage has long been established and could be the result of evil spirits drawn to submissive subjects. Women recently wed have been known to whisper throughout the night and to dream of splendid fish seeking entrance to the moon. Women deprived of husbands will gibber and babble, or mouth foreign languages. Also, it has been established that young girls may sprout hair by the age of ten and at twelve go raging after a man, but how this latent force emerges I know not. So might we look in vain for the source of a mighty river. Why concupiscence would thus manifest itself seems beyond understanding and without bottom, like a Portuguese harbor. Lust seems as imperious as the flame which orders everything aside—burning dwellings and forests, withering lakes. Actaeon the hunter when he surprised Artemis bathing was caught by the hounds of his own distracted thought. Endymion wished to sleep forever on the slope of Mount Latmus that he might re-visit Selene. How does perversity restore us? Are we inclined toward what we oppose? The animosity of love I would compare with the fly Cantharides—golden wings affixed to a body indurated by poison.

I WONDER that men marry nymphs, which are threatening because their intellects and minds preserve the similitude of our own and through us they become immortal. But still they have not immortal souls, so any man who would take a nymph as his wife must be careful neither to offend nor insult her, nor abandon her beside the shore of a lake with her crisp hair glittering, because she will vanish into her element.

MEN and women appear to rejoice at correspondences of form, much as dissimilar things move toward each other to embrace. Yet there is one pleasure of a horse, another of a dog. Cattle differ upon their choice. Arguments persuasive to one to the next look unconvincing, even as that truth acceptable to Hans may seem offensive to Kurt, according to temperament or training. Therefore, if like is to meet and act upon like we anticipate concord, whereas if the actor and acted-upon stand at sword-point we look toward contagion or virulence. Often there will be wrath and bile, just as we find in plants an herb or vegetable furiously engaged against its neighbor because their constituents are less a unity than a multitude. Nature seems disposed to act in the same manner if furnished with identical materials, whether to reproduce monstrosities such as the mule which issues from a congress of ass and mare, or beings conformable to their particular species. Some insist that mules are born on a distant isle and as to their genesis we know little, but I suspect that with judicious proportion most things may be accomplished. Also, we stand more in need of holistic physicians than apostles. Ah! I would give advice that sounds helpful when I myself do not understand. By God, I walk in fancied circles.

I DEBATE what nature hopes to achieve with us. Could it be an escape from incogitance, out of vacuity toward entity—shadow to substance? So do I question the admixture of evil, by what warrant this pervades a room, what is its composition and how it mottles the lucidity of thought. Raveled in doubt I comb the constellations for one favorable burst of light. Orion walks poised and balanced on pinnacles of diamond fire while I am grown full of device drawing together metal bones. Where is the alchymic root or spring? What might be disclosed should the lamp illuminating our universe prevail?

HUMAN intellect enables us to choose among contrary paths, but how should we decide on the parabola of thought? I have looked toward the radiant arch of understanding only to observe a net built with entanglement. Yet, it is critical that men discover how presumptions originate—with such vehemence does the mind influence the flesh, since we are conjoined of two laboratories—corpus being that which tangibly labors, whereas the intangible we describe as imagination.

SHAME compels the face to blush, fright summons pallor, ague, trembling diarrhoea and melancholic obstructions. Envy evokes jaundice. Delight stimulates. Sadness oppresses. Intolerable anguish contributes to miscarriage, hysterics, apoplexies and malformed children. Of this, as of much else, I am persuaded—as by his thumb alone would I be able to recognize Hercules. But how does the simple bird conceive her nest? Whence comes the prosperous wind? Why should a circle lack angles?

WHAT is the provenance of those glorious hues that engage us during spring and summer? If we consider the gross nigritude of earth it proposes nothing fragrant or savory or desirable, nonetheless iridescent colors emerge along with a plenitude of living creatures—shining pools replete with an infinity of fishes, gracious birds, leaping animals—amid a plethora of minerals and sparkling stones such as emerald, alexandrite, carbuncle, girasole and peridot, all derived from abhorrence. Out of an herb yclept Colorio when it molders in cattle dung crawls a most repulsive larva, yet as its carcase is burnt— Anon! We behold the rainbow. Who can attribute the mysteries of nature?

EARTH appears to be the premise and foundation of all things, constituting fundament or centrality, at once the sole object and recipient of heavenly beneficence, proprietor of seminal virtue which, by stimulation, attempts to reassure and liberate that which it is offered. I have heard it likened to the belly where matter digests itself in order to be renewed since every shape represents the tomb of another, which is self-evident and a determining precept of creation. But I feel apprehensive about confining movement to parallels.

I ASK about the maturity of wheat—what obligates it to grow. A seed must be planted in soil which encourages it to secrete the essence dormant within its husk, whereupon it flourishes. Now since that is so, what inhibits a multiplication of gold? But let us say the matrix should be disqualified for humidity, or too much or too little of some other aspect should develop, then we would feel surprised because nature objects to change, although like a generous mother she rewards that husbandman who meliorates his ground with compost, who scorches weeds and resuscitates morbid matter through fructifying unguents. Hence, the alchymist beginning his assault against disease by accoupling observation with intuition should anticipate a fulsome harvest. Yet I have watched men mark their schemes out of obduracy toward fatal excess.

IT IS clear how vegetables resolve to expand beneath the sun, but when they think the sun too strong they decide to perish. So should an alchymic doctor apprehend the tendencies of heat and cold, of moisture and desiccation—of every debilitating operative and seasonal monarch. He must not bitterly complain how what proved useful or effective once must prove effectual twice, but should assiduously chart the progress of sinister blemishes, learn why cinquefoil despairs and follow the seven proud daughters of Atlas—Celaeno, Electra, Sterope, Taygeta, Alcyone, Merope and Maia—nightly plotting their trajectory, because we embody a universe comprised of mortal and celestial spheres. Consequently, if a man's organs neglect their office he will fall sick, he will lift up both hands to providence.

MANIFESTATIONS of disease and health fluctuate because Sol and Luna which now travel separately once were affiliated. Thus it follows that as sidereal objects decline or ascend a patient's condition will appear to deteriorate or improve. We should note also that expressions of agony characteristic to the moribund often disappear, which suggests that paradise might not be far distant, closer than we expect.

THE BODY submits when it knows it must, if mortal flesh admits no alternative. I have heard Chymists suggest how resurrection is possible when substances containing Harmoniac are supplied—charcoal, wax, oil and soot—which seems implausible. Illness desires its medicine just as the man desires a wife, this much I accept. But what argues our claim to restoration?

I KNOW that we estimate the size and shape of a dog or an ox or a tree by its shadow just as we estimate degrees of health or sickness by inspecting the quantity and color and odor of urine. I know also that nature will announce the perfect way and order without which nothing can be done or brought toward a perfect end. So much I admit, yet the earth may be compared to a scaffold upon which each individual is required to stand alone, where each determines his future.

$\mathcal{S}$ALT, Sour, Sweet, Bitter—these four savors a body accepts, but how often foolish men misapply the fragile cup consigned to their use. We have been offered a cornucopia of pleasures such as spiced wine to accompany our meals, music urging us to dance, friends for conversation, illustrated manuscripts for enlightenment, docile beasts, et cetera. Still we expend this provender immoderately by giving way to intemperance—raging against our fate—unlike animals which do not doubt themselves and thus live comfortably. Subordinate creatures refuse to eat or drink injurious material, selecting instead what nutriment they require through natural instinct whereas men yield to gluttony, swallow foreign liquid, make flatulent speeches, load their bellies with carnage, defile themselves, rake over the world and succumb to grief.

$\mathcal{C}$ONSUMING sanguine barnyard flesh is perilous because it rots and makes wind, thwarting rectification of the blood, whereas the meat of birds is salubrious because these creatures subsist upon aether—the noblest constituent. Legumes are believed to accumulate their strength from diurnal quantities of sunlight which is released into our bodies, hence such plants are good and do not inflame choleric humors. Solar foods are beneficial to humanity, for should any organ conflate or grow distempered others miscarry—as if the fifth string of a musical instrument should be tight or loose. Now, because this is not mysterious I feel puzzled that the less knowledge blundering doctors have the less they covet to know. Myself, I would not maunder about as I hear others do, hiding ignorance or flaccid uncertainty behind confident prescription. I would as soon dance the jig with some itinerant minstrel or frolic in the hay with goats. I regard this earth as an infirmary, and I am but one earnest doctor in search of the Great Catholicon.

Spurious physicians stroke their beards while hawking unguents extracted from tragacanth, verdigris and fat—as a mendacious moon does falsely tint familiar objects to make the gullible exclaim at counterfeit spectacles and rejoice and clap hands, thankful to sensory illusion. Honest practitioners seek truth in spiritual verity, reason in moral certitude.

Receipts and magistrals past counting have left us unequally perplexed, but through systematic observation various matters which astonish us may be resolved, lessening our amazement. Aristotle writes upon a Greek afflicted with defective vision that caused the atmosphere about him to act as a looking-glass while optical streams from his eyes, being reflected backward, threw forth an image of himself which faced and preceded him where he walked. So do most men agree to mistaken adumbrations for the probable semblance of themselves, inanimate and hollow. Did not Olympiodorus mention a natural deficit to understanding? Did he not speak of conceptions that lie askew?

Van Helmont discusses an old woman cured of noxious megrim by a touch, and he speaks of an abbess with a distended arm that could not bend her fingers for at least eighteen years, but she recovered by the application of lictus to her tongue. I think humors as qualities in themselves do not exemplify health, being little more than conditions neither indigenous nor natural. Bostock asserts that these might not be a cause so much as caused. Perhaps. I subscribe to several minds.

IN THE city of Frankfort is alleged to be a Dominican by name Uldericus Balk who employs a magnetic analeptic for jaundice or dropsy which is made from five drops of a sick man's blood rehabilitated in the shell of a speckled egg. Being fortified with animal meat and set on the ground before a famished dog Balk's lincture acts vehemently against disease by expelling it out of the patient and causing it to reappear in the creature—much as that leprosie in ancient times passed through Naaman into Gehazi. This seems possible. I myself effect sympathetic recures by a withdrawal of blood to attract mumia. Extraction through cupping, plus venesection, ensures an adequate supply which is given to a surrogate after boiling with onager milk. Even so, I judge the comportment of a doctor more efficacious than his remedy, more puissant than his finest drug.

I THINK disease results from an overflow of corrosive catarrh which descends from the base of the skull to visceral organs. If fluid reaches the lung we may expect apostema and phthisis, in the joints we anticipate rheumatism and gout, in the legs ulceration and decay. Such ailments derive from the treachery of malignant or idle planets—which is commonly acknowledged. Nonetheless, it seems that by admitting the physician with his corrective, providence has imagined and conceived of balance.

Surely a subjunction of astronomy with medicine directs us at our labor because we have seen duplicated in laboratories a macrocosmic circulation of celestial agents that resembles falling rain or the pulsing motion of blood. Venus and Mars and a red moon in trilateral opposition revive old disorders while new configurations of Saturn introduce fresh disease. What is the attribute of Mars if not aetherial modes of iron distributed broadly down the progress of nature? And Venus? The power to stimulate vasa spermatica in masculine bodies. Or what is Melissa? We know it to be a subtle astral essence choosing materiate expression in the humblest garden plant. Or what is some animal if not a personification of sidereal human characteristics? Page after page therefore illustrates universal correspondence. That being so, terrestrial events must derive from the absolute harmony of heaven since beams of starlight fall indiscriminately across the earth. And as the nature of light is to flow continually, without respite, what fugitive phenomenon could be out-cast?

If it is verified that stars have both their amicabilities and enmities, being given to mutual attraction or repulsion, each withdrawing or venturing toward an area of its neighbor, such coordination could not exist but for conscious empathy. So does Roger Bacon argue how those luculent encrustations that like a cascanet of jewels embellish the fluctuating and fruitful matrix of this earth have grown up in response to everlasting agitation among angelic properties. Myself, I believe it vain to endorse or question seraphic philosophy. I would sooner ask the nativity and circulation of pestilence that in distant lands flaps down men like flies.

Francisco Giorgi comments upon inestimable steep influences which pour ubiquitously out of heaven across the receptive surfaces of earth. I see in this a most marvelous neutrality, yet I notice how many seem inclined to moralize and grapple with fright if planets recede or advance, if new stars glow at the horizon, if comets lose or gain luster. Why is this? Do they fear what happens below or that omnipotence above? I am unsure. Angles intersect.

Khunrath explains how the universal medium of preservation and restoration shall be the Regnant Child which by its own equilibriate virtue contrives to expunge mortal suffering, thereby rectifying both provinces—both of corpus and mind—depending on the capabilities of each. But I would sound out first a cause. I suspect impurities adhere to their substance. I think acidity weakens the spleen, sugar expands the kidney, grief sours the lung and salts encrust the heart. I observe quick-silver trembling in the aludel. I watch menacing seeds sprout. And there is strange emptiness behind the moon.

Porphyry has argued that life's wheel deviates from its axis so that our consequence must be dissolution. Now death betrays a duplicate structure—one which men understand where the body disassociates itself from the soul, but another comprehended only by philosophers in which the soul feels emancipated. Therefore, no physician should look to advantage in gold, nor intermediate benefits, searching instead for merit lest inimitable unities be denied while the source of the fountain flow undiscovered.

𝔙ERULAM believes that by replenishing the impulse and vital principle, vis vitae, a corpus may be rejuvenated. Perhaps. Like planets that men invest with fancy, they are one thing, men's image another. Thus it becomes a habit of metaphysic to ring changes about our Egg—around and about once more—with each note and cadence varying. All the same, very little turns smoothly for its song. So many men, so many opinions. Suppose we should burn a tree, enclosing ash, smoke, vapor and every other component within a cucurbit, adding to this a living seed. Will the tree be able to reconstitute itself? Yes, it will. But without the seed could it be vivified? No, because the principle of a plant does not subsist upon ashes nor upon smoke, but within the restitutory Mysterium Magnum from whence it must be urged to reclaim its vital semblance, endowed with qualities it once possessed.

𝔖UPPOSE a child lovingly retained the sperm of his parents, would he not duplicate their configuration? Yes, of course, just as a pine tree is anxious to recreate its predecessor. Hence it must be commingling that makes the son to diverge and become estranged—to reject the sound of his father's foot-step, to withdraw from his mother's affectionate touch. Why does he fail to acknowledge superior regents? Upon what miscalculation would he admit no governance except his own? I account men's souls equal but about their operation I note perplexing diversity.

THOUGHTS that I conceive—are these mine? Or, being universal, do they but await apprehension? If the latter, then innumerable ideas exist which I am not able to grasp, as stars are created or extinguished at such a distance that men pass by oblivious. And the provenance of stars being infinite, like that of ideas, how does the realm of perception end?

IN MY judgment the mind resembles an instrument focused upon delicate inquiry, and therefore man is driven to the resolution of puzzles. I have myself stood amazed to see silver burnished with ash of basilisk duplicating the magisterial gleam of gold. I have watched a birch tree cringe when the axeman approached. I have heard a violin register living torment with every note. I have listened to the yowl of a starved bitch discourse upon the largeness of suffering. Thoughtfully I walk back and forth like the god Morpheus with his horn and ivory box of dreams.

MY UNDERSTANDING is altogether tenuous, incomplete. Even so I have been persuaded of very much. I think minerals succeed through the transference of radical moisture and vegetables through some increase of efflorescent activity, but animals attempt to profit according to the exigencies of their being, because all things yearn for a nutriment to which they grow accustomed. Surely this is true, but why? Stones must fall, boiling water evaporate. What further leverage is required?

WHAT causes a seed to produce its fruit? Sponginess within the soil, which was authorized by heaven so that atmosphere and liquid succeed in finding access to the interior flame which presses up through earth's core. By this inosculation are humid vapors subtly exhaled which corrupt or decompose the germs of things anxious to regenerate themselves. Thus each prepares and welcomes vivification.

I THINK atmosphere might be a vital or pervasive spirit that begets both life and substance in men, encouraging and fulfilling, which is why I consider it not an element but a providential glue or a medium to provide coherence. And because it retains attributes of celestial mobility it is able to communicate with sleepers, disturbing them until they groan and twitch in dreadful efforts to escape while struggling against the mighty import of divination. That is why men dream. But as to why obsessed individuals dream with the impetuous desire of those miniature comets which flame across August, I do not know. I regard these as stones graven according to heaven's face—Gamahei.

IT SEEMS apparent how nature was not meant to be comprehended but acts magically. I cannot say why the dandelion that blooms at seven enfolds itself at five, nor why the pimpernel withdraws at night. What encourages such dissent? Were not both nurtured by soil and aether and sidereal radiance? Or how should the dog shake his tail when he is pleased but the lion if he is angered? What urges things to put forth their hidden attributes?

W HAT governs private intermissions of the heart? I have seen mongrels envy and bite each other just as men cull and steal and dispute and choose violent satisfaction, so all together become what they profess to despise. Then is this mankind's republic? Out of the universe, seeing he was thus constituted, what does he anticipate? Who is he—this anomaly that forges iron like wax? I read upon his visage the look of ascendancy which is both awful and undecided.

L IKE Ezekial upon his dream I am full of wonder. Fundamental antipathies and sympathies coalesce to hinder man's journey, as thistles do not flourish next to figs, nor grapes beside thorns. On the contrary, toward each must be the most exact and perfect intent, each according to its kind. Yet I notice how often men will select paths which diverge one direction but also another, so that they turn distraught and querulous and toward midnight reaching for a pillow they find a stone, by dawn mistaking dung-beetles for gods.

I BELIEVE that mankind subsists of four dissolving elements. Nevertheless, works fluctuate as do their private mercuries because calcination secures quick-silver and every imperfect body during disintegration fulfills itself with philosophic precipitate, which is mercurial water. What dissolves the sun dissolves also the moon, and harmony results from the analogy of opposites.

Should the mid-day sun be collected underneath a hollow glass it will focus its effort to burn inward with terrible passion, yet the burning rays from a human heart provide no discernible warmth. How is this? If astral coordinates achieve equilibrium I think the heart might generate and distribute adequate fluid, but if balances have been disrupted the corpus succumbs to drought, so variable and importunate is this devious organ.

I suspect that blood resembles wine during its slow process of development. I would compare infant blood to grape-juice before fermentation, while that of an adolescent resembles fermenting Must. No doubt the blood of the aged is complete, liberated from harmful ebullience. Why, then, would old men expend themselves to gain frothy titles or deposit gilt paper in paper kingdoms? Each merits his scallop-shell of rest.

Atoms of blood presumably are round and smooth, gliding past one another without discomfort—in contrast to those of iron, which must be harsh and coarse. Atoms comprising a soul I imagine to be gelatinous or immature because of unfulfilled promise. Atoms of flesh must be formless—inert and sluggish. As to the brain, I suspect its particles are nimble, elusive. Philosophers argue that we should not speculate like apostles on substantial employment since time works about us, quilting and scoring innocence. I myself think arguments of philosophy more fatuous and sterile than breezes ruffling the North Sea. What sick man hearing them ever shook off his grievance?

I PRESCRIBE long ocean voyages to counterbalance enervation because water serves as a powerful adjuvant toward phantasy, but if asked to explain this animus—I cannot. Or by gazing toward the wintry shoulder of Albristhorn I willingly rejoice with little comprehension. Hapless I reflect on my beginning in a yellow cloak, a student burrowing at darkness, an unread apothecary calculating circles by a cupping-glass whose vitals quaked at the sight of green wounds. I think I must be very far from the lap of eternity, stippled by pinchbeck rhetoric, Arabian conjecture. I am an alchymic doctor at the rim of the world and five days have I traveled without a compass.

I MARVEL that innocuous physics be administered while the rich rioting with extravagance weigh up possessions and multitudes languish outside the Mineral Gate. If motion be a quintessence of its compelling impetus, upon what authority should mankind anticipate the new dispensation? How shall we watch amber and cassia and rarities cast up to the shore?

BY WHAT logic is the frog ugly? Was he not formed to express the nature of his inwardness? Therefore what man is deformed or vile or delirious except through a listener's proclivity? Or how is any cleric served to preach and condemn in public if not to herald the commencement of idolatry? I would ask for the names and titles of six high priests that by virtue of their faith shook mountains apart to drive misconduct out. I ask how we could identify Satan except by his limping gait. Was this consequent upon man's spiraling plunge from heaven? I would gather the purpose of Aramaic and Latin and Hebrew—if such tongues have been employed to praise diabolic agents. I would know what pseudonyms have been spoken by the Karcist lifting his hazel wand in the magic circle between two arches. Gnostics say divinity's key was held by a snake that apprised us of its understanding, so how does grace penetrate any man dressed with disguise?

WHY a rubiginous toad simmered in oil cures leprosy I cannot decide, but it is apparent how evil welcomes evil, which explains why a toad sucks venom from phagadenic ulcers. Worms may grow inside a walnut despite an impenetrable shell just as malignancies are able to gain entrance and threaten a contented body, although I find no reasonable explanation. It seems obvious that apoplexies, convulsions and lethargies feed upon transient humors engaged by disaffected particles of thought during sleep since accretions evolve in solitude. But what accounts for this? If I do not know, what else am I than a farrier sporting the doctor's miniver hat?

MONKSHOOD plant, jasmine, tutia, camphor, mustard, pepper, anemones, passion flower, chymistry, sophistry, automata, logic, barbaric medicament, astronomy, exorcism and ancient craft—with so much am I familiar. Invigorating substances are known to me, or malleable metals that shine and ring. I could speak of pulverized resin, camel hair, bone marrow, luminescent ink, agents inhibiting rust. Clancular poisons as well as piss display their qualities like Japanese iron without pretext. Were it not for the introspective physician who should prescribe a treatment appropriate to humanity's requirement? Now why were men granted two ears but a single tongue? That they might speak half as much as they listen. So it seems incumbent that the doctor rather than vomiting forth ignorance should pause to justify his prescriptions. I know how Botanus Europeus if applied to gangrenous ulcer must be submerged in dung and left to rot, since otherwise the malady suppurates. But why this has proved efficacious I am unable to decide. Nor can I explain how mercury heals that which it provokes. Why should arsenicals do likewise? And as vinegar is stirred into milk we note the separation of heterogeneous material into its elementary constituents, implying the inseparability of creation from degeneration. And since I have grown burdened with doubt I embrace doubt, that first rung on the ladder extending perpetually upward to wisdom. Knowledge makes a sharp scythe, I think.

PEOPLE hearing that some alchymist could not multiply gold or has failed with his attempt to restore a sick patient—they exult, they say it could not be done. But the peasant whose crop was parched by drought, is this not identical? Only providence decides the moment when closed seeds unfurl. Now if the patient who accepts medical advice is observed to recover, it suggests that his physician was sent by God. Yet if he does not, this also is a sign. Inadequate doctors ripe with certainty abuse and ravage, whereas the initiate acquires facility through meticulous readings. I know very many things are inveighed against Theophrastus and very much I question his logic: how each skill or craft derives from God, how by faith our imagination be perfected, how sidereal effluents drip from above, and early portents signal early death—as planets shook before the crucifixion. Such sophistry gnaws against my being. I do not trust it. Yet by the magic of disciples his name persists: Alexander von Suchten, Leonhard Thurneyssen, Oswald Crall, Gerhard Dorn, Melchior Schennemann, Adam von Bodenstein and Peter Severinus—to say nothing of Fludd, Crollius, Rheticus, Faber, or the chymist Jan van Helmont. That he confounded pedagogues is established, ocean fish do not seek a river. Critics quaking with envy claim he brought little relief to arthritic old John of Leippa who lived then at Cromau. And John's son Berthold, whose gross right eye he treated, went blind. Also there was a baron's wife wracked by colic who turned epileptic because of therapies he administered. Thus they expect to count his worth, jackasses which snort and paw before the harpist, fools forgetting how frangible complexities trouble the progress of art. Judgments drift, we oscillate among rainbows.

M Y THOUGHTS tumble—rolling and bumping, pebbles in a tide. I know not how considerations be held inducible to reason if we are caught up by the net of love, music and flowers. What appears erroneous or doubtful may disclose its origin unwittingly since we were born at all adventure, because what fate prepares for us seldom reflects our expectation while the mind plays toward what it desires.

Perhaps we do not see what we think, but as memory suggests. I have watched how moonlight prohibits leaves from stirring and how Noctambulous about his journey seeks communication with departed spirits. So the night offers access to unknown riches generous with imagining until what logic cannot teach we quickly apprehend. And I believe there is a private craft to the manufacture of dreams because this sounds reasonable, just as it seems clear how leguminous diets or a superfluity of fermented liquid may be the cause of frightening visions at midnight when responsibilities do not constrict the brain. Often it is said that eunuchs and celibates forget to dream, which I doubt, as I doubt that violations of moral authority inhibit sleep. But if so, what follows? Consider how Gabricus approached Beya as she slept, only to feel himself swallowed until the Stone of the Self withdrew. Therefore what is Beya except mercury? What is Gabricus except sulfur?

Eudoxus has taught how Jupiter concealed himself, ashamed by his deformity. Then out of compassion Isis appeared and stooped to separate the entwined feet, thus restoring him both to himself and to society. Well, returning to a thing must imply that at some previous time we departed from it, consequently I wonder if we adumbrate the shape or spirit of tomorrow. Saturn tells us plainly how matter is created, annihilated and born anew because he devoured his children in order to spew them out, but where this leads I know not. I have become one that struggles at night against anonymous antagonists. I despair at insistent riddles. How does nature impetuously generate showers of frogs? Why does the carcase of a mule give birth to locusts? How precious metals be cast underground by the exhalations of rejuvenating mineral vapor I cannot explain, nor why men genuflect to shadows—toward what covenant. Hermetic nights do I consecrate to magistery, to imperative questions. I munch wort leaves. I strut forth reaping strange fields.

I HAVE observed venomous creatures crawl out from moldering festering material, dependent not upon their natural parents but necrotic waste, hence subject to fraudulent duplication by unscrupulous adepts: scorpions, maggots, slugs, hornets, red ants, spiders, midges and brendels—invidious eidolons begotten with the assistance of reflective morbidity. False mortals devoid of souls have been propagated spontaneously, figures conceived independent of terrestrial mud, fashioned from dissolute spermata—sprites and nymphs, fairies, giants, gnomes, scrats, pygmies. Priests would incriminate Beelzebub for miraculous contrivances, or Behemoth since he is the lord of blasphemies, or Isacaaron and Leviathon which are agents of lust and pride. It is true that satanic deputies could be responsible, but I have seen crafty barbers extract bloodied glass shards from the distended bellies of groaning patients or sticks with clumps of hair, and needles and ivory buttons. How often I see common motives serve uncommon events.

I NNUMERABLE enigmas we attribute to Satan and call them his handiwork which are but consequences of natural philosophy, such as Alexander's Pillars that are a monument to ambition, or the Caspian Gate whose iron bars Hercules could not bend, or those columns Caesar built at Rome by the hill Vaticanus, or those crenulate peaks mariners have reported which thrust steeply up from the Western Sea that are called antediluvian watch-towers. I wonder that we should look to phantasmagoria above fundamentalities.

Beelzebub's apostles are alleged to debase and mislead men by masquerading as rocks, trees, cats, black lambs and owls, occasionally posing as delightful children. Also, it is said they seek out continent nuns. Perhaps. Testimonials flourish. But I suspect illness inhabits the brain as well as the body, and unlike our prescient sun that reads the sky for guidance I believe men seldom direct their course. Where do we look for counsel if a robin taps at the window, if a pullet crows like a cock, if a jackdaw flies down a chimney, if circling ravens alight on the church steeple? Let metaphysicians wrangle. I myself exclude necromancy, conjuration and all demonic partnership from alchymic therapies, because I am engaged with this craft for good, not to the prejudice of living things.

According to monks, the Prince of Darkness assisted by ghouls suspends fertile maidens and lusty youths from oak branches, binds their inverted bodies to stakes and boils their flesh in cauldrons. I wonder at this. Also, regarding the disposal of plague corpses—especially those of sodomites, harlots, thieves and maugre chirugeons—whether these be devoured or discarded, I cannot decide. Physicians debate in themselves. On few matters am I positive, but the recollection of birth and an expectation of death lurks always within and makes us separate, so that we find the taste of humanity intoxicating, delectable and precious.

I HAVE heard that images buried under stones by necromancers cause the intended subject to feel oppressed and lethargic, so that he lies helpless until the onerous weight is lifted. Or if a magician should twist the likeness of an arm or leg until it wrinkles and breaks, then will a similar infirmity be duplicated on the hapless victim. Or if a copy is stabbed or burnt or disfigured with acid, this too shall be repeated. Why so? I think it happens because our spirits act in concord. I believe all things establish their colony.

EACH individual is permitted to live out the existence nature assigned, therefore who should decide to protest or object or complain against lives pulsing contrarily to his own? The pulse of granite is not rapid or brief while that of a horse is variable. Whatever is ordained cannot be dissuaded from its usage. Why would we inquire of the rose where it blooms without prickles?

IT MAY be that nature subsists upon this agreement: flowers, insects, animals, birds, minerals, fishes, herbs and trees have their parts so qualified that nothing seems homogeneous, yet all creatures have their class and each variety aspires to its own estate. As a tree with buds, leaves and branches is at root one, and as the leaf survives the exhausted bloom, or the trunk without either was made to endure a frigid blast, so do all things manifest their quintessence in this respect, independent yet complimentary, neither more nor less.

𝕴ᴛ ɪs obvious how each presence—flower, thorn, metal or worm—cannot but exhibit some virtue, albeit less than the planets which deliver our light and governing intelligence. Selenite is a divers stone growing purple or green or oftentimes white that we pick from the bosom of Indian snails, which if tasted will provide hints of future matters. Sapphire also is a rock that traveled to India out of a mysterious eastern provenance, which adorns itself with suitable colors, the most prominent being luteous—engendering rapport, devotion and concurrence—so that any man who wishes to feel at peace should grasp it. Amandinus is a rock prodigiously formed, enabling every man to overcome his adversaries, or to prophesy and to interpret and expound upon dreams while unraveling difficult questions. Also with Chelonites, which is found inside a mollusc's head. If a man place this under his tongue while the moon comes up he will forejudge and conjecture upon swiftly rising problems. Also there is one called Adamas, which the English have named Diamond, with a very sparkling color and impossible to crush, that is rumored to grow in Cyprus or Arabia and being bathed in the blood of a goat it will fracture—from what inadequacy? We know not. Despite this I think nothing can exist that fails to hide within a recess some private impulse or significance. The constituence of tin, for example, seems disproportionate because its mercury may be fine whereas its sulphur is corrupt, and since a commingling is thought to occur between the layers this metal is heard to shriek. I have met men so commingled.

ALCHYMY employs stone to alleviate Stone—crab's claw, lapis lazuli, eagle-stone, selenite of Judaic—since out of these we procure a calcined excretion which dissolves more quickly than salt in heated water. Distillation enhances our deposit, providing the essence of restorative balsam. Yet those virtues resident in every panacea, congenial to many, prove malignant and damaging to others. The salamander dips himself in fire, the peacock hungers after serpents, the ostrich swallows rock. What good to them are humanity's nutriments? What men consider instrumental, sacred or wondrous may prove deformed and untrue. Let us ask if the workman that acquires his important illness from a lead mine should be purged with circulations of galena or by cathartics derived from its opposite. Ash of the burnt cray-fish—Karkinoi—is this not effective against carcinoma? Has not every path some ultimate turning?

HOMEOPATHIC principles conspire to surmount disease even as outward aspects of medicaments define their usage. Eufragia, which endeavors to duplicate the appearance of the human eye, directs itself sympathetically toward this vulnerable organ. Thistle, which seldom hesitates to attack the hand, assuages interior stitches. And the root Satyrion, that orders itself to the shape of mankind's generative part, restores virility. Hence I think it unwise to discard that which providentially invites inspection. Nevertheless, I have met physicians with no more brains than a dolt at a banquet who lacked wit enough to stick the game in his mouth. What they fail to comprehend they damn. Speech is granted to all, intelligence to few.

Celandine, tormentil, burnet, eyebright, pimpernel, rue, heart-trefoil and lovage genuflect to the command of Sol, even as lettuce, colewort, arrach, fluellein, loosestrife, pellitory and saxifrage subordinate their lives to Luna. So do bourage, chervil, hyssop and melilot and cinquefoil render obeisance to Jupiter. Bifoil and fumitory comfrey, mullein, woad and darnel relinquish themselves to Saturn. Beneficial partnerships frequently develop between heaven and earth—this is beyond dispute. Now whether the passion of an herb may resurrect the departed, we know not, nor if exaltation by the soul revivifies the body. If so, hermetic medicine exemplifies precepts betrothing science to magic. Might we be induced to live again? Who can say? We are sure only that familiar animals such as the bear renew themselves after prolonged sleep, while houseflies and wasps stupefied by frost grow nimble once they are warm, and aged hawthorns that for decades have languished will proliferate and bloom as though they were rejuvenated. Hence, the ponderable world represents a simulacrum, or palimpsest, of all that subsists invisibly—as with portraits the feature is not truly shown but takes up equivocal shape.

Very little out of fiction does a prudent alchymist credit, but states honestly what he considers reliable and positive. Should he grow hesitant or feel uncertain of his diagnosis, then he abstains from counsel. But should he feel persuaded he will abjure equivocation by publishing and disseminating whatever he has learned, thereby reflecting honor on himself in accordance with the compassionate majesties of his craft. So it is incumbent that every doctor proceed on experiments with their contingencies. Suppose one neglected to appraise the ebb or flow of macrocosm, how would a physician estimate the frequency of feminine menorrhagia? How could he predict the course of bloody flux if he failed to identify the source of showers, detect the humors of colic if he did not follow the wind's birth backward toward its grotto? For innumerable gifts we receive we feel obligated and of these the fairest must be a propensity to reason. Thus, with Saturn ascendant under a full moon, having removed the heads from two spaniels I affixed them by intricate sutures to the body of a third, and contrived with praise, stroking and constant affectionate encouragement to preserve the similitude of life until dawn. The inferior head remained conscious. It seemed by a yearning look to approve, as though it might again participate in life, while the superior head displayed neither sense nor activity. What this reveals is doubtful, but where nothing comes to pass nothing keeps its shape. This being so, enquiry continued. Inside a stoppered bottle I placed twelve new-born titmice exactly at sunset, recording how they shuddered and twisted from lack of sufficient aether before submitting to fate. Also I have macerated the bones of tiny birds, and sliced apart fish bellies to probe toward the secret fundamentals of matter. Yet everywhere I meet that mysterious serpentine line traced by the hand of some incomprehensible presence. What else have I learned save the imperious ring and pulse of insistent life?

PLAGUE! Plague at Lübeck! Plague preceded by a bluish veil or cloud visible from Bremerhaven. Disorder. Tumult. Panic. We are told by Johannes Nohl that teardrops trickling down cathedral walls and blood-stains on previously immaculate garments betoken this curse. A dragon swimming up the Tiber proclaimed a similar visit, according to Gregory of Tours. So did ash hurled from Vesuvio. No doubt. But as with twins which manifestation has gained its likeness from the other? Cosmic emanations that presage catastrophe stream toward us while mankind looks to the ascendant—to a fresh and binding regeneration. Now rising news of peste like a wisp of basil breeds scorpions in delirious minds. Let the Lamb keep time, evil marches west. I think we may anticipate a trumpet blast with terrified calculation on the number of our days.

I WONDER about the impulse of this scourge. I disagree with de Chauliac who would assign it to conjunctions of planets by which the atmosphere and various elements are so altered that poisonous fluids gravitate toward internal constituents of the body just as magnets may be observed to attract iron—from which arise frenzies with bloody sputum and depositions in the form of glandular edema leading to suppurating boils with agonizing death. Varro believes in a subtle provocation of inanimate creatures, which would explain the degeneration of susceptible organs. Kircher argues how spontaneous worms capable of flight upon being sucked into a receptive corpus by motilities essential to a lung might conflate the animus, vitiate blood and gnaw flesh apart, which I think reasonable. Agricola points to especially turgid aether that originates in putrid exhalations stemming from unburied corpses, notably those of mercenaries that were stabbed or died of starvation. Might stagnant lakes, caves, or miasma from swamps be a cause? Or possibly the atmosphere is corrupted with excess moisture through prolonged rain and fog after a warm spring when east winds prevail—resulting in a plethora of flies, gnats, lice and other deleterious insects through involuntary generation, these being known to transmit humors. Or the comets of autumn emitting morbid exhalations. Or infectious mice. Man himself could be responsible if excessive emotion unites with sinful imagining. Yet like an arrow this Black Death strikes toward three vulnerable locations—ear, groin, axillae—suggesting that its impetus be external. Possibilities multiply. Doctors stand helpless, weak soldiers that think to demolish a castle through musket shot. Myself, how might I know what to believe should I grasp at the counsel of others?

THEY say plague walks to the accompaniment of a rushing noise followed by toads, snails, beetles. Moths fall upon vine-yards, cats huddle unnaturally, dogs forget to bark. Oily rain falls, hideous flowers open. Women swathe their bodies with sheets, men lurch to the burial ground. Mountebanks employ juggling and musty relics—counterfeit miracles. Downward the spirit wheels, sucked beneath contrary tides past the secret glome or bottom of our days. Thus it seems self-evident how mortals squeeze more from rubefactions than albefactions—drunkenly circling, gesticulating, depositing goods on mon-astery steps although every portal be bolted by monks glazed with fright, sequestered against eternity. But what exercise of privilege is there to holy office? Gold coins hurled across the bulwark echo unpleasantly through God's enclosure. So many demonstrate their low dimension, refusing to help the moribund and argue how Necessity supersedes our mutual bond. Yet as men permit others to fall they disparage the given franchise, arrogating to themselves a prerogative of divinity. Conscience I ascribe to those fundamentals we are offered, according to the dictate of which each should act without inquiring as to its purpose. What we are taught, that we do—so have men been instructed. Otherwise we look at reflections of emptiness.

How and by what method could this pestilence be contracted? Some assert that like dust it accompanies the wind, lodging where it pleases as do worms in fruit. This I think unlikely. Others point to contagious vapors drifting north from Egypt, which sounds plausible. I suspect vulnerability occurs during effervescence when the blood decays after furious attempts to expel turbid, foaming redundancies. Also, children whose organs lack development readily succumb to epidemics and the reason is clear: Inadequate or excitable blood distorts the veins of adolescent bodies. Yet if asked, I could not answer which illnesses be justified. Who among us would judge the hind part of God?

Regarding prophylaxis, the air being swollen with effluvia should be broken apart. Violent noises usually are helpful, such as the explosions of cannon, ringing of church bells, and snarling dogs. Sulphuric bonfires might be appropriate to correct the humidity by restoring an equivalent balance to consonance, because this scourge very possibly emanates from atmospheric distemper. Interior and exterior surfaces must be sprinkled with vinegar in order to weaken virulent atoms. Spiders should be encouraged to devise complex webs at every corner, subduing evil. Fresh baked loaves of bread displayed on a stick absorb toxic influences. Curdled milk on a window-sill or outside the door is a sovereign panacea. Bezoar and hyacinth-stone show equally admirable properties. I think the breath of oxen is salubrious after midnight so these animals ought to be tethered inside the dwelling, but should not be eaten since turgid meat proves dangerous. Suckling pig is unhealthful, as is the flesh of waterbirds. Any food which is cold, moist or slippery could be harmful. Bathing might prove fatal. Intercourse promotes diarrhoea, which is debilitating and conducive to melancholic apathy. Heirlooms made of gold or silver assuage the troubled heart, hence these may be regarded as prophylactic by untutored or fatuous doctors. Nonsense! Many times have I seen the beard and cloak while the analeptic I doubt. Yet what am I if my experience stands useless? Very often I have no idea what to prescribe. Perhaps we are governed by atomi within the seed.

CONCERNING treatment, a poultice of figs and boiled onions mixed and simmered and mixed with fresh butter ripens styptic buboes. Leeches assist. Theriaca of snake may be good, or the rectum of a predatory bird macerated in chyle. That suppurating boils be cauterized with rods is preposterous, resulting in little except discomfort, albeit Guy de Chauliac reports twelve lives lengthened. At times I think most treatment less efficacious than eating night-owl eggs or pissing through a bronze ring. I consider it wise foolishness. Infirmities seem our fortune. These visitations that beleaguer us—I suspect they descend from above and our eyes open to a pitiless world where mirage begins.

Black Peste has leapt the Rhine. Theology falters, violence ensues. The muzzle of a black rat scurrying through darkness darkens with hate while we feed on terriculaments. Fright writ like letters on a map where topographers label some territory Unknown. And each victim, calling his anguish unjustified, begs to be excused. Earth rest lightly on the unfortunate.

Outside the Bruges Gate at twilight this vagabond, his paunch puffed tight like a woman full of triplets, groaning piteous, dropsic from leaking buboes, all corrupt and red foamy lungs, swelling myrach with a blue flame flickering out of his mouth, gibbering, whining past bloody teeth, a stink like swine gall with a goose honking at his feet—none knew why. Blessed I am that I have yet to meet an imitation of Christ or a disciple selling such restrictive faith. I suspect the true Alchymist might be providence, our security and light.

What benefit to congelation or sublimation while the visage turns mottled? What purpose distillation and cupellation? In a mirror I see not myself but Ourobouros.

Ola! Thus accosted by an unctuous Spaniard stroking a tidy mustache, velour cap overlaid in gold with a yellow feather, velvet upperstocks, pantafels and pynsons, with a satin cape hanging from one shoulder and a purse slung about his neck, sporting a gilt rapier and the luminous gaze of a sewer rat who swore he could produce the Infant—which secret he might barter for a trifle since his good wife had but recently died and he lacked funds to dig her grave. One drachm I displayed, bidding him exchange it for tickets to paradise. We are close, he said, very close to a beginning.

Rumors of a wandering magus conceived in heresy and mistrust that would resurrect us . . .

How often we hear that natural species may not be transmuted because one into another means spurious descendants. Hence, adaptation of gold by lead must constitute gross inadequacy—the superior species defiled through admixture—which results not in corrupt gold but, according to their harmonic virtues, gold of a middle synthesis. Now this objection we acknowledge, although it appears to contravene both science and the Adept. Yet here is a misunderstanding born, since we do not endeavor to transmute species, nor do we teach how inferior specifics such as quick-silver can change to gold—no more than a dog should live again as a pig or vice-versa, or anything unlike. Indeed, it is but the primary substance and radical moisture of which things uniformly are comprised that we would extract, transporting through craft a lesser to a greater constituence. Thus we demand of Skeptics: how should one effect transparent glass out of lethargic flint, ashes and stone?

Foreign riches accrue at foreign places, and being Scribes have we compounded divers records of successful transmutation from Lesser Egypt to the Baltic.

We DEPLORE those that calibrate reconstitution by their wit and so doubt miracles of hermetic art—objecting about gold how it could not be present within copper, nor silver within galena. Should imponderables be weighed upon their balance? We point out that birds issue from eggs, while caterpillars develop into butterflies. We observe particles of the element water extant in wood, since heating fresh wood begets liquid. Similarly must wood be the home of atmosphere because we note vapor and rising steam, and because we find ash there is earth. Hence, any substance might be transmuted through proportionate realignment of its components. Therefore, what is the Skeptic but a new mouse fumbling through darkness?

We REPORT how substances boast the germ by which they flourish, but among metals—excepting gold—this germ resists maturity. Therefore, all these must anticipate decomposition. Skeptics will cling to their philosophy, the incredulous to incredulity. We decline to quarrel. Who would provide mirrors to the blind or entertain the deaf with music?

We ARE persuaded that lead would turn to gold, granted time, since no metal is conceived immaculate. Nature intends first to create the imperfect, distilling and by degree distilling until she accomplishes perfection, as we observe when beetles or wasps charged with strength crawl out of rotting corpses—

albeit misbelievers complain there is fakery, and claim gold could not survive in dross. Yet wise nature labors upward to consummation. Accordingly, the agent to promote such changes must exist. How else could we explain that sweet tractability of blossoms emerging from the rigid husk of insensate seeds? And the phlegmatic worm—what drives him to enclose his body, ultimately to unfold translucent wings?

THAT the Magnum Opus will be accomplished we have no doubt, since God bequeathed His knowledge of alchymistry to Adam through the medium of Raziel by whose grace it was offered to Enoch, whose preserved bones rest in a private apartment of Cheops' pyramid. And this authority we no more question than we should analyze the mounting architecture of clouds. O, we have listened to merchants discourse at their stalls how spagyric art is but some thaumaturgic dream of wealth—a vacant invention drawn up for simpletons, vainglorious trumpeting, implausible rubefactions. In fact, we hear them dispute under the nascent moon if its diameter be as great or less than that of a cartwheel and amazement overcomes us. We wonder what should distinguish men from transient shades except the alchymic dream. We wonder if they be not deceived by their own infirmity. Which among them would fix one hour toward the health of his soul?

WE RECORD how Meister Sendivogius achieved his inimitable work before Rudolph the Emperor by converting quicksilver to gold with the aid of negritic dust—attested by that marble tablet affixed to a wall of the room where transmutation took place, bearing this inscription: Faciat hoc quispiam alius quod fecit Sendivogius Polonus. We have listened to disbelievers object and argue, but like blackbirds which start a tune well enough they do not go far with it. We consider them foolish that turn with intolerant haste from authentic art. Monsieur Desnoyers, that once was Secretary to Princess Mary of Gonzaga, testified for the validity of this inscription. Still, cautious scribes take note how the dust or powder may be either red or black—since we are told by the alchymist's steward that this was so. And he carried it in a miniature box, and with but one grain he could make five hundred ducats or a thousand rixdollars. And when he traveled he gave the box to his steward to carry on a chain slung around the neck. But most of this black dust he kept in a secret niche carved into a step of his carriage. And foreseeing any danger he would dress up himself as a valet and mounting the coachman's seat he took the place of his valet who rode inside, and so they proceeded. And to every question we respond by asking if each gelle of water that passes a mill need be verified by the miller.

We note how Jean Delisle, blacksmith and native to Provence, when he acquired the Philosopher's Stone permitted visitors to witness an elevation of imperfect mineral to perfection—this miracle attested by M. de Cerisy, Prior of Chateauneuf in the diocese of Riez, who without delay notified the Vicar of Saint Jacques du Hautpas in Paris, expressing his delight that a substance which for generations was thought chimerical had been distilled by a neighboring blacksmith in the parish of Sylabez who could without the slightest difficulty refine silver from rusted buckets and bring forth gold from shovels. M. de Cerisy asserts that now in his possession he has a Nail which is half-iron but half-silver, which he himself created under this blacksmith's supervision. Scholars write in Latin: Ecce signum. What further proof is necessary?

Now the physitian Arthur Dee, who was off-spring of Sir John and intimate of Sir Thomas Browne, swears he played at quoits with gold plates that his father once projected in the garret of their lodging at Prague. And he claims how at various times he examined the Philosopher's Stone. And says about his father that he did often clarify the shells of eggs—for what purpose he never learnt. And we hear that Sir John was much discussed by the playwright Jonson, who called him Alchymist. And also one Robert Cotton alleges how Sir John did conjure up a pool at Brecknockshire from which a slim gold wedge was fished out. And he could build a mighty storm above, or eclipse the moon, so children dreaded him. Whether such examples be guaranteed is moot. We do but put forth events as they occur.

Being dutiful Christian secretaries we record how Sir Kenelme Digby meditated very much in that he had a most candent mind such as would rake across India, and composed numerous books regarding dark science, and by the help of sympathetic powder which he rubbed on whatever instrument had caused some wound he would cure that injury. Also, he was quite diplomatic while commanding sailors of the Navy during which time he annihilated both Venetians and French. Also, we have heard how during a masked ball the Queen Mother Marie de Medicis so improperly advanced on him that he fled and escaped to Italy. He was gigantic, altogether handsome, and employed graceful elocution which made those knowing him insist he had dropped to earth from the clouds: Lapis lapsus ex caelis. Being counted a Royalist he loitered around prison at Southwark, there strangely diverting himself with formulae which enabled him to transmute many valuable stones—emeralds, sapphires, rubies and the like out of common flint. But also toward the end he came to resemble some hermit with his beard unshorn, and grew faint with debt, wearing a high-crowned hat and a desperate long cloak and would converse in six tongues. That such a life be well or poorly spent exceeds our quarter, being resolved to keep account for men of notable disposition with promiscuous curiosity.

CONCERNING the illustrious Jean de Meung, we have inspected twelve-score musty documents establishing how he issued from a noble family, practiced the arts of astrology and chymistry together with poetics, gracing the court of Philippe le Bel. That he was interred at the Jacobin Church we have no doubt, nor that to these monks he bequeathed a granite cyst, begging their forbearance till the service of his death be concluded—a request they declined to honor, impatiently raising the lid to find not what they expected but a somber library of slates scratched with indecipherable geometrics which antiquarians interpret as a disillusioned parable of our Savior's promise to unify mankind, since for this miracle no date was ordered. Now who shall look on the glass of divinity or tell the hours when to rain? We have most thoughtfully read this masterpiece of Jean de Meung, titled by the alchymist Romaunt de la Rose, in particular those verses 16,914 through 16,997 that withhold from humanity's intemperate gaze inestimable directions toward fulfillment. Very many will ask the end of hermetic subterfuge. Excellence, we respond, is not cheaply sold.

We could with Pineda in Monarchia Ecclesiastica attribute to 1,040 ancient authors our fountainhead, and so retrieve neglected matter like those magicians which draw up birds or little dogs out of smoke. Arnold do Villa Nova, Ficinus, Reuchlin, Lull, Picus di Mirandola—neither disbelief nor obloquy diminishes the grandeur of their art, as centuries of verdigris do but superficially tarnish Palestinian bronze. Lustrous disquisitions leaven our bleak and perilous extremity.

Have we not forty-two works by Hermes which are both exigent and useful? Thirty-six encompass the vast philosophy of Egypt while six pertain to medicine. Concerning Muslims, Albusarius relates how wisely they have preserved with occult translation the magisteries of Chaldea. Anagogic teachers out of the past enlighten us. We might take to bed by candlelight a Spanish Jew, Isaac de Moiros, Synesius and Theophilus and Abugazel that were African, Alphidius and Rhasis and Rosinus and Hamuel that were Arab, Pontanus that was Fleming, Hortulain that was Scottish—some say English—Gui de Montanor that was French, Pierre Bon de Ferrare from Italy. To an impetuous river of compelling logic all contributed. Still, what is the worth of scholarship, given moral inferiority? Does not every age and place make up a world for itself? Now why so?

Because the fruits of elements diverge according to place and time. What good has balsam to provinces remote from Arabia? What value to Leipzig has Rhazes, Arnaldus to Swabia? Enough! Like Asiatic sultans that would go hawking after butterflies with sparrows, we misappropriate the hour.

MEISTER Boerhave speaks on some adept whose name is long forgot that brought up suroxydized muriate of quicksilver, promising to catalogue the fusibility of mineral. Many assert this to be Abou Moussah Djafar al Sofi, born to a genteel family of Haman in Mesopotamia. Others allege he was native to Thous in Persia. Scholiasts would with Xerxes flog the Hellespont to submission. We, as conscientious archivists, disdain such strident music, restricting ourselves to the simple nobility of fact.

WE TAKE note of a solid gold mortar unexpectedly disclosed when the ancient quarter at Kufa was demolished and Al-Azdi's work-shop stood revealed. We think this artifact must symbolize inimitable abundance. Yet what was once good does not remain so perpetually. Decadent, surfeited, men reach out to brittle and cursory ideas like pilgrims that linger to fondle glass leopards in Musselman bazaars.

LET amanuenses bred to the exercise of pedantic study register how Mohammed-Ebd-Secharjah Aboubekr Arrasi after three decades squandered on musical composition exchanged frivolous pleasure for recondite medicine and philosophy. His treatise on mineral elevation he presented to Emir Almansour,

Prince of Khorassan, who generously replied with a gift of one thousand gold dinars and the request that he provide a demonstration for the Court. We find parchments affirming that this attempt was undertaken without success. No precious minerals resulted. Then the Emir attacked the alchymist—belaboring him, striking him brutally so that he went blind. Nevertheless he lived to be one hundred and died impoverished after writing two hundred and twenty-six illuminating manuscripts. What is alchymistry but an incomplete volume without words? What is it if not a mystic rose—a petal of the cosmic flower?

WE ASK ourselves what of that Musselman pedagogue and chymist Jabir ibn Hayyan with his exploration of acids and varnishes. We marvel at such a copious brain because we read in Aquarium Sapientum how if a man responding to any gift vouchsafed him by Allah should wax covetous—then will his gift slide apart as though it were not his to keep, sliding out of his grasp. And wonder assails us how so little wealth could be recovered from furnace ash—one gold turnip seed to validate the Opus. Such trifling evidence disturbs us. Might this be the extent and culmination of joyous labor? Was it only to philosophers that Dame Nature accorded her secret for compounding wealth? Jabir ibn Hayyan expired at Tus with the Book of Mercy beneath his pillow, a matter which speaks for itself. Ah! Once again we digress.

NOW we have learned from Suidas how the Emperor Diocletian ordered every anagogic document burnt at the public market, thinking thereby to thwart or obstruct Egyptian alchymists whose skill at confecting gold levied troops against Rome. By his odious act Diocletian attempted to extinguish an art, which we believe constitutes rape against our sensibilities, and each event cannot but leave to posterity its eviternal trace or pattern.

Does the raging sun spiraling overhead exult at our progress? We suspect vainglorious men inscribe their histories on some codex rescriptus. We point out the prophet Zoroaster rejecting all men save those avid for knowledge, who lived on a mountain behind a curtain of celestial fire. Then appeared a mighty king accompanied by his mightiest lords and all of them supplicants, and the prophet came out of the fire to greet them, and prayed, and offered a sacrifice on behalf of Persia. And when his body was consumed by a thunderbolt they vowed to preserve his ashes, but thoughtless descendants neglected this office. Subsequently the empire declined and broke apart and contributed to an earth already corrupt its ounce of corruption. Unless through parable or sign, what declares a truth? We ourselves, being indifferent to wasteful metaphysic, simply record the ascent or decline of remarkable days. All else we bequeath to the hand of a majestic Overseer.

We have known hermeneutes penalized for their simplicity, yet we watch them move close to God. And what mockeries they make against us may be hurled back upon the world at Judgment Day. Olaus Borrichius points to the lightning flash that disclosed a manuscript of Basilius Valentinus concealed within a pillar of the abbey church at Erfurt. Now, whether this be construed as a meaningless inadvertent eidolon or threatening apologue and reprimand, we plead much ignorance. As pious secretaries we devote our thought to Christian cosmography—being mindful that when Jehovah descends to judge and to censure or praise what we have done He will follow a conflagration like a pillar walking across the hills from the sea with dazzling radiance, and those that look to the core will fall down blinded.

Recently have we made a most arduous journey to Fulham Church that we might view the sculpted sarcophagus of Sampson Norton where inexpressible disciplines speak privately to the initiate from shadows cast by marble foliage. There did we contemplate with quiet satisfaction the cockleshell atop Saint James' hat. And we reflected upon that Musselman, Geber, whose perplexing symbols angered and mystified this world of avaricious mortals disposed to incontinent dreams. And we recalled of Harpocrates that with one hand concealing his mouth he represented secrecy, which is sustained by silence but with revelation grows weaker until the emblem vanishes.

We doubt it could be an intent of art to enrich the illiterate or sacrilegious, no more than flatulent mechanics be ordained to shear and sack and market the Golden Fleece. What merchant is appointed to benefit through harvesting and selling baskets of luminous apples from the Hesperides? Why would we vouchsafe to brutal minds what they could not interpret? We reflect upon Jakob Böhme wandering in a cave at Old Seidenberg near Görlitz who saw at his feet an ivory coffer overflowing with coins and rubies and tourmalines and emeralds and sapphires and pearls. And as he told his companions about these riches they wondered that he took nothing for himself. And flinging up their hands because they were blind with greed, they rushed into the void where reverberations of emptiness met them. Then full of rage they charged the philosopher with delusion. By virtue of this we see how the ambitions of artless men prove turgid. We note their hostility to a benevolent mind. We register with sorrow the paltry nature of their concept.

WE HEAR of a lamp in the tomb of Cicero's daughter Tullia which has flickered without interruption since the regency of Julius Caesar, nurtured by some liquid defying analysis. And we have inspected a burning lamp excavated near Alestes inscribed by the hand of a forgotten Roman: Maximus Olybius. And we have been informed of the mystifying Bononian Enigma. Now we are told of Hermolaus Barbarus who comments on water known to ancient hermeneutes, depicting one which is divine or ethereal, called Scythian Latex, that expends its spirit laboring toward the absolute distillation of liquefied gold and is alleged by Khunrath to burn with serene persistence. This we assume to be that irreducible thrice-blessed elixir by whose light the Magisterium illuminates eternal tenebrity while disclosing nothing.

How should the Adept prepare his lodestone of bodily health and temporal felicity? There is but one method, as we learn from the Sophic Hydrolith. One catholicon must be recombined with nebulosity after purgation, the fulfillment achieved by Pontic Water which is more luminous than amethyst or diamond. Thus did Noah construct an ark, Moses a tabernacle, Solomon a temple. This was how a golden snow wrought by Vulcan's art fell on the city of Rhodes—which is not the gold of vulgar pharmacists.

WHY would a Novice scatter precious hours on fugitive wealth if he has been adequately instructed? Thomas Aquinas laboring at imperfect matter informs us how metamorphosis is plausible because we discern no autonomy in the government of elements. But he would direct enquiry to a higher purpose than elevating the mineral republic. And we approve. Conscientious historians distinguish lovers of mammon from lovers of truth.

NOW we learn of beakers filled with gold traveling from fire to fire at the laboratory of some Cambridge professor called Isaac Newton. Essences are said to grow outward like branches but through continuous circulation are persuaded to dissolve. This we compare to the craft of a skilled geometrician who by one stroke from his compass could describe a right line, yet rather traces a circuit or a different path. Mayhap our foreign chymist goes chasing the nonexistent light. Mayhap he defines no miracle superior to the next nor believes one element subservient. We ask what follows that could accord with the discipline or gospel of mystic art. Basil Valentine reminds us how a man with a quantity of flour will make dough, and he that has prepared dough will find his oven to bake it. Now we do but register with absolute fidelity what we collect, feeling content at the shape of the leaf.

Rare news have we regarding a parchment scroll from the hand of Thomas Charnock measuring eleven English feet in length by nine inches breadth, uncovered at his house in Comb-wich. It is said that six panels of the entrance to his work-shop were painted by this alchymist with very ingenious emblems, al-beit coarsely drawn and tinted, suggesting some equivocal re-lation to the Opus. Also, by the hearth lay an instrument of queer design which he would use while attending the fire. And there is said to be a very ancient woman that remembers his daughter who supervised the work, but neglected her task one warm night so the flame went out. Charnock's experiment seems forgot although many suspect he had cast a Brazen Head which was prepared to speak. Now such deformity could occur, we admit, yet as cautious scribes we make our reservation.

Are we not streaked with imagination among rudimentary idols? Do we not join sects and cultivate doubt and sow misbe-lief? Are we not dissident, vehement? Are we not quick at judgment? Pelican, ambix, aludel and retort. Trowel, tongs, sand-glass, drug-jar, croslet, beaker, sieve, bellows, spatula and funnel. Filter, pestle, mortar, crucible, flask, athanor, Phil-osophic Egg where art is born—upon this premise would we circumscribe the intersection of mankind. Bred to fractionate accumulations while riven by the pulse of life, squandering power on useless urgencies, invidious, undecided, men at their quotidian labor fly back and forth, winged seeds tossed by con-trary wind.

BEYOND the circumference of flesh how do we meet satisfaction? Plato, on his discourse regarding colors and tastes of water in rivers and seas, explains that perceptions vary by concord with the earth through which it flows, taking up every weight and molecule—transgression and deviation—much as the soul varies according to the temperament of its body. Consequently the motive for our universe is justified because the existence of each living thing has been affirmed with moving qualities. This we applaud, hearing a most admirable music.

WEIDENFELD exclaims upon those innumerable gifts vouchsafed from above—which we do not hesitate either to acknowledge or reiterate day and night by consenting to the jurisdiction of our Lord. And as we are not loath to accept His blessing we have been called microcosm. Now, this estate we consider most excellent. We think it unlimited. How should men avoid the lees and puddles of earth on private initiative? Hence, Nature withholds from avaricious chymists Lapis Philosophorum toward which the future bends.

PLOTINUS has explained how wisdom arrives swiftly by itself and brings with it an empyreal universe where entities seem diaphanous, while matter asserts itself to human faculties, living resplendent in each particular. Now since the majesty of God is intense and splendor radiates, what is untutored becomes great as the moon and sun and stars blend together.

WE ARE TOLD by François de Foix Candale, Bishop of Aire, how comprehension of celestial matters surpassing that allocated to Hebrew prophets—equaling that of apostles or evangelists—was acquired before the advent of Moses by Hermes Trismegistus. Further, we have heard Khunrath, Böhme, Freher, and Grasseus testifying to metaphysic art that not merely antedates but corresponds with Christian orthodoxality. Being pious notaries, we ask how the pure might be severed from the unholy, since God bestows grace wherever He decides—overlooking all that plead or beg. Also, we question the source of misbelief. Does it arise complacently out of ignorance? If so, we seem consigned to live doubly helpless since we exist not only unaware but incapable of departing from ignorance. Accordingly, we compare ourselves to a corpus indurated with disease which, oblivious to its torment, seeks no cure.

MEISTER Tymme speaks of an Almighty proffering two ineffable volumes. And the wisdom of this first, which we call natural philosophy, urges us to exalt the produce emanating from our Savior's hand, since He is in-dwelling—the efficacious cause toward which matters tend. But the wisdom of this second book opens upon subterraneous cosmography and therefore is closed to all save seraphic minds.

MEISTER Böhme declares that as he was born to the similitude and image of the Lord God he has opened but one single text. Like a child in its mother's house that requests no guidance he bent himself to this restorative volume, excluding others, since as he looked to the palpitating surge of his own heart he understood the armature and structure of the world.

Now, in that model of the universe drawn up by Meister Fludd we notice an ape shackled to a woman representing celestial harmony, who is herself shackled to an inimitable presence beyond our sight. Thus are we linked to heaven with a chain, yet apostates argue that man is satisfied to emulate nature, content with senseless mimicry, exchanging forgotten dignity for immoderate power. This we dispute. As didactic historians it seems to us that man beset with trivial endowments must be superior to a discarded husk—greater than a mummified rind broken on the surface.

IAMBLICUS argues how the tenuity and attractive subtility of divine guidance is such that initiates might be affected in the manner of fishes drawn upward through dense, turbid waters toward the luminous radiance of a higher atmosphere, only to become deprived and languid and sickened—forsaking the connascent spirit which directed them.

PYTHAGORAS notes how we seek a light, exemplified by angels, when we speak of God, so that during journeys through prayer and convocation we carry a candle to refute those obscurities which accumulate with darkness.

FROM the Anonymous Pedagogue we learn of a prodigious book in which our Lord has communicated such truth as we require for adequate knowledge of the world and of His high majesty. This being so, who should cry out? We do but change position, twisting like victims of plague which endeavor to alleviate their anguish. Is it not wiser to let stars shine through us? Afflictions beyond reason entreat the spirit to suffer calmly while in a darkened antechamber the body waits.

ARTEPHIUS, with his learned work on humanity's predicament, has endeavored to explain that transcendent process whereby all men shall pass through the discipline of God and nature out of chaos toward unity. So we find our heavenly roadstead charted with its various coasts and bays—how the land falls. So would we indict heretics that, like stolid contented oxen licking their noses, do not appreciate Genesis. If not oxen, what are they but monkeys dressed in silk?

NOW, as the tree was adorned by our Lord with succulent fruit so did He burden the human spirit with an exuberance of shapes and ambitions toward knowledge. Therefore, we ask of the mole what does it signify in his blindness? Might this be a papist reluctant to admit the folly of his course? Or with Patricius we ask whether oceans roil above the sky. Also, we would learn how it is that gold spent by the wise, stamped with lightning, glistens pure and clear. And why should yesterday perplex men with unrequested answers? We are distressed by all affections which plentifully doubt the geniture and scheme of existence since all matters descend from His hand. Still, as registrars we dedicate our season to metaphysic service. We fat ourselves with present joy as a glutton slips toward his dish, a satyr his harlot, the credulous his idol.

FROM Hugh of Saint Victor we learn how the dove's two wings represent the active and contemplative lives of Christianity. Next are we taught how the blue color of her wing signifies Heaven. The shimmering, soft nuance of her body—tremulous and inconstant as the sea—exemplifies a passion threatening our vigilant church, about which Mankind must thread its path. Behold those grasping red claws that betoken an ignoble world saturated with the blood of martyrs. Behold those yellow eyes, what do they represent? Thus are men consumed with unfulfilled desire, gnats drawn to a candle.

WE ARE taught by the hermit Morien that he who lusts toward superiority encounters no abundance surpassing his own self, while the orb of this earth reveals no greater excellence or mystery than the humble figure of a common man reformed by our Lord into some other image. Yet, should the aspirant be not himself purified and cleansed and aged by the labor of experiment—much as the subjectum with which he works—why should the measure of his ordeal be preserved?

ACCORDING to Thales there is but one world which demonstrates the construction of God. Metadorus argues otherwise, claiming a universe populated by numberless worlds since their causes must be numberless, which contention we reject as sophistry. Who has not felt the obstetric hand of God? Who can mistake the light for its ray? Light is the cause, brightness the effect.

WE HAVE studied how four elements representing a Quaternarius grow entwined with their indecipherable Ternarius and Unity during the incarnation of our Savior. Hence, three plus four make seven, that Septenary a Sabaoth into which the creature enters. Therefore, we suppose transmutation with resurrection must be equivalent. Yet, for no two men are events identical and the springs of behavior lie hidden.

WE HAVE looked upon the considerate spider assembling his web more efficiently than a man and have watched the industrious honeybee manufacturing a house more artistic than any palace, so we conclude these must be blessed insects, albeit assigned to trafficking with fungible goods which decay or degenerate. Man by himself goes ranging across the night and neither Luna nor Sol shall direct the course of his study.

SOME endorse the stars as instruments of unlimited authority, intermediaries that influence us yet neither seduce nor abduct nor deprive men of opinions which formulate their inheritance. Nevertheless we are at first deceived by what looks virtuous—much as the light bequeathed us turns mutable or shifting.

SEPARATE subjects have separate truths. According to Meister Franciscus Picus, men watch approaching events through a mirror governed by benevolent constellations and built in compliance with natural laws of perspective—which Friar Bacon would name Almuchefi. Now, this may happen as we are told, but mayhap not. Often with great fiction some claim they were there to see it. Being as we are but didactic amanuenses, we look to divisible success until the prophet be modified in body and spirit.

WE ARE informed how a wreath of Sinechrusmontes Behdem encloses the deadly glass encircled by blackwood sticks which harridans arrange, which they float upon buckets filled with lake water and expose to a nascent moon—whose image reflected upward must radiate downward, because a poisonous oval infects the earth. This proves how the atmosphere is able to convey foul influence, and how the vindictive contaminate spirits other than their own. But as conscience becomes a tablet on which offenses are laid up we ask how amoral souls persist in the moral universe. What is the agent of such audacity?

WE ASK if Jehovah delights in righteous adherents. Or is this a mockery, a conceit? We wonder why Johannes de Rupecissa perished in a Vatican dungeon for experimenting with prophecy and denouncing the future of nations—twice visited by Etienne Aubert, Innocent VI. That evil arrives dressed with a bright and sudden gaze, we doubt not.

OR WHAT of one that sprinkles the Paschal Lamb with sour herbs? John Wierus comments on a villainous magistrate assisted by princes, dukes, demons mistitled marquis, counts and accursed presidents congregating for heinous intercourse—frightful spirits who negotiate apartments in temples while praising obscenities. And we are rolled up with obedience and no viceroy shall exist above that dominating a man's mind. Or do things freely combine through submission to one regent?

We ask if humanity's requirement be some fabric or synthesis—a morality it cannot live without. Much discourse have we heard of Albert von Bollstaedt who beckoned white magic to his side, constructing an automaton imbued with the authority of speech, which he named the Android and that like an augur fastidiously served him by responding to every question. Now, this we call perilous because the distinctions between good and evil belie their intent, nor was a man meant to compete against divinity. That is why his pupil, Aquinas, picked up the hammer.

This monk we have titled Doctor Universalis since he has taught the quality of common plants in Liber secretorum Alberti Magni de vertutibus herbarum and has instructed us with De Secretis mulierum et virorum on the aspects of male and female mystery. And with his ultimate labor—Compendium theologicae veritatis—that was printed at Nuremberg, Frater Albertus unveils a world of metals and minerals, of mechanics, of compounds, of physics and of chymistry, not to mention eight hundred lesser subjects, by such industry preserving the marvels of Arabic scholarship. Nevertheless that diabolic grimoire embellished with talismans extolling the Ring of Invisibility which was flaunted at Lyons—Alberti Parvi Lucii Liber de Mirabilibus Naturae Arcanis—this is a wicked misleading book quite untouched by a masterful hand, hence it must be considered spurious. Thus would we compare him to our Stone replete with beauty, both inimitable and worthless, disguising what is evident. His corpse we are told was exhibited at the central quire of the Dominican convent where it resisted corruption. His entrails we believe were carted off to Ratisbon where once he served as Bishop. Now, all this we think merciful so we entreat our Lord on behalf of a learned servant.

𝔖KEPTICS demand to know what mortal is qualified to serve God. We answer without hesitation that because He deplores impurity nothing might exist in His presence which is vile or blemished or compounded. They ask what of Agrippa, who expired face-down. We would not deny that he ordered ducats out of slate, nor that the obedient poodle trotting at his side was meant to advise him of distant occurrences among foreign people. Further, we do admit he died with his face to the floor at the house of the Receiver General, which is on Clerk's Street in Grenoble, in the province of Dauphiné, and that his black accomplice drowned in the Isère—ending an illegitimate search for knowledge. Yet, like the blind that gaze wrong directions we feel reluctant to decide. Ignoring Satan's rhetoric, we believe that a compassionate God looks down with indulgence upon troubled scholars. And we demand to know if there be not numerous doors to the temple of knowledge.

𝔐EISTER Heinrich Cornelius Agrippa with wondrous felicity and limitless eloquence could translate or dictate eight languages while conversing upon every subject. With admirable integrity he has explored in his gigantic work, De Occulta philosophia, how the impassioned commitment of but a single soul directed through imagination may benefit and guide our faint majority. So we ask of skeptics what rate seems usurious?

FROM the great canon of Jean d'Espagnet, Enchiridion physicae restitutae, we learn that God was a book rowled up in Himself that enlightened only Himself before the universe was created, but unfolded Himself during travail with the birth of a world and brought light to the womb of His own mind by extending it to mortal view, so the world was framed with immortal extreams. And in the sun was the center of the world. And in the center of the whole was the sun, as the considerations of nature and equity seem to require, since the body of our light should have equidistance from the dark fabric of the world and the genesis of its fountain that it might receive an abundance of strength from its chief source and upon like distance convey this wealth to a universe below. Are there not many kinds or forms of unity? These are good and licit and commodious things which we hold up toward the looking-glass of reflection.

ANDREAS Libavius explains with his masterwork how spagyric art shall consist of perfecting magistery by extricating essences from a coalition of bodies through exceptional multiplications of imperious matter. But say we are descendants of Adam born wretchedly to ashes and dirt, how shall we persist in seeking that which we lack the wisdom to hold, or vouchsafe ourselves a constellation of faculties that we fail to exhibit?

We have heard Meister Eirenaeus Philopones Philalethes contend in The Marrow of Alchymy how our subject is mercury associated with gold, both decocted until neither forsakes its opposite, so that both rot and putrefy—giving up themselves to glorious regeneration. Now, this finest of seven substances we identify as Monarch which septic fluid does not contaminate or necrotic soil corrode, since it was regulated by nature. Hence the King embodies nothing superfluous. Therefore, we grant this mineral supremacy and propose that it dominates lesser metals, flaring like Sol among weak planets, and by the production of mercuric gold from miserable atoms our Lord completed His majestic work. Thus, if man is the noblest creature it follows that he manifest some divinity which cannot be corrupted.

According to the Dutchman, Meister Isaac, if our Regal Infant transmutes one million times its weight into meritorious gold we have demonstrated the Magnum Opus, and all that obediently accept their allotment shall endure until an hour God assigns. Yet we watch indifferent men gossip and work toward their aims all oblivious to the parabolic curve which hurries them apart, bones washed in wine, huddled upon glyphs and numbers, saluting vacant air from squalid littorals, histories close-writ across the chapbook of iniquity while persevering at vengeance—fools eternally plowing the desert, extolling a long and witless jest, ignoring the prodigious fulcrum God exerts against our world. How shall they anticipate redemption? As conservative notaries we decline to speculate. We do but stock-pile fact.

Hoeksters would ransack occult chronicles for those pro-
cedures Saint John employed to benefit the impoverished and
to assist the decrepit by confecting silver and gold. Disparate entities coalesce. Where one predominates the consequence shall appear elliptical, but where equilibrium prevails a
circle results—as Jehovah's hand hurled the stars into perfect
courses.

May not the close of a motion be also its beginning? Yes,
since things turn upon their pattern, returning to no end other
than their own. Therefore we believe in palingenesis. Avicenna,
Cardanus, Averroes, Eckhartshausen, Seneca, Plato, Caspalin
and others confirm the truth of this. Athanasius Kircher at the
court of Queen Christina resurrected a rose from ashes.

Now, because we are humble biographists expending ourselves with quiet scribbling to complete the archives of inheritance let us consult that emerald attendant who swallows his
tail—Ourobouros—the serpent exemplifying mystery to be
devoured and melted, transfigured by dissolution from its first
estate to one of inimitable gold.

Look! Ah, we behold some malodorous, greasy-visaged
trickster disguised in a Jerusalem beard creamier than milk and
a gown befitting a penniless wizard—ripped silken sleeves
spangled with glittering stars with a half-moon smiling on his
breast, the cowl pushed back from a face to make poor Lazarus
faint. And he has brought his scrying-disk of polished cannel
coal and a globe to manipulate which commands disembodied

spirits until they swarm quicker than bats chattering for entrance. Now does he fill up his pelican flask half with yellow seeds that should be mothered night and day like a squatting hen warming her clutch of eggs who would hatch out golden chicks. God speed! We doubt he will usurp a throne nor surpass Midas except by the length of shaggy ears. Therefore, good passage. We cannot guess what formula he offers. With each disposition nothing travels swiftly save toward itself.

Rumors of a wandering magus conceived in heresy and mistrust that would resurrect us before the gates . . .

TIME unfurls, buried images out of joint. Souls
mortgaged to grievous error. Ideals pass, titles follow.
Priests withdraw, casting back morality. Ash begets ash.
Truth legislated from existence. Gold thickens.

LILIES shrivel in the moat,
crops cease to flower.
Providence justifies catastrophe.

RED Prince astride White Stallion.
Mercury and Pisces conjoin.

SPIRITS bound to dead forms rise. Credulity
displaces inquiry. Reliquaries
buried in a wall.

Malversation. Murder.
Archduke admires double phalanx.
Councillors applaud.

MUNICH. Verdict unsealed.
Corruption. Pravity. Famine. Mucor.
Penitents clog a muddy road to Augsburg—
gesticulating, mumbling, singing. Wafers molder.
Recidivous prophets riveled with debauchery cavort,
weeping, desecrating the book of revelations.
Hans Böheim shrieks. Vacuity embraces firmament.
Comets wander. Apparitions swarm down hollow streets.
Darkness by noon. Two suns divide, bending inward
darker than a wool-sack. Nazarites genuflect.
Manuscripts unroll drenched with blood.
Palas aron azinomas! Agla! Tagla!

CONSTELLATIONS mount, opposed armies descend.
Sister of the White Rose stumbles.
Crime in lofty places.

MONARCH appeases monstrous daughter. Battle divides,
concessions astonish. What is to come boils
unobserved. Pillage. Sword.
Foreign sails. Antiquities crumble.
Black fleet approaches, lives forfeit.
Withered grove. Stony field. Blazing village.
Janizaries defeated—hurled aside. Cattle bellow.

𝕱IERY path, charred corpse.
Sightless peasant.
Which hand shall touch perfection?

𝕸AJESTY hesitates, false credenda mount.
Doubt troubles cathedral. Frenzied voices trace
oracles to Zoroaster, Eleusinian mystery to Orpheus.
Loathsome fraud. Apostles gather, pretenders act,
difficulty bristles. Aged regent slumps,
gibbering. Throne aslant.

𝕹IGHTWATCH.
Drums.

𝕾ALAMANDER. Arcturus deliberates.
Anguillae sequestered.
Terrier hanged.

𝕯RAGON to devour luminous wings,
periods of earth bound in water. Marvel
predicts the future. Candle flares—
four fingers ignited! Beryllisticus advises.
Hand of Glory resuscitates.

𝕱IRST ballot.

𝖁ENAL city destined to perish.
Say we do not feel cunning
with logic or wise in aspects of stars

175]

or sublunar things. Say we do not see causes
nor observe them at their rising,
how shall we put on salvation's garment?
Say more are damned than rescued,
is not the devil sovereign?
Theodonias! Anoor!
Amidas!

WHAT predator hears the shriek of its prey?
Priscillanus the first heretic
martyred. Cecco d'Ascoli
sacrificed to necromancy. Johannes
Mercurias da Corregio pacing the boulevards of Rome
crowned with thorns. Sabbatai Sevi unveiled
as the Messiah. Francesco Pucci
beheaded. Bloody flesh
smoulders on the Campo de' Fiori.
Bruno immolated—wedge between his teeth.
Pico conspires to unite religion
with philosophy. Guseyn!
Abaddon! Marbas!

REVOLT in Calabria. Charity declines.
Campanella preaches. Eight less nine plus
seven angers six. Sceptered Moon
escapes, water surges.
Red Servant bows.

COZENAGE scours the earth. Deep tides
mount. What is to come reverberates emptily.

Serpents entwine. Castles for gifts. Chamberlain
opposes the polychrest. Minatory cries.
Mutable face. Orderlies prevaricate,
spirit withdraws. Destruction.
Necromantic mage.

MONGREL returns to vomit,
washed sow to mire.

MORALITY inverts. Unrest.
Disorder. Diabolic ministrants.

SECOND ballot.

ARGENT strangled.
Moon-calf jousts with authority.

GRAY Lion awakes, trembling wind.
Triune mitre flecked with blood. Nuberus.
Worms of the marrow.

STARS bend on their track,
judgments harden.

NO PAST but inhabits the mind.
Say the present is Sol, the past Sulphur,
the future Mercury. Present answers
neither past nor future. Then what is second
with respect to the third? With respect to the second
what shall be third? Quick-silver shudders

in alembic. Iscariot. Bishop recants.
Malfeasance. Obliquity.
Merlin summoned his future
to avoid the past. Kraken. Raven.
Manticore. Six upon six
upon six!

MEASURES of iniquity exceed their limit.
Shrieks of the oppressed reach unsleeping presence.

KING enfeebled by pox. Magistrate
emerging from fire rejoices at his espousal.
Wealth accumulates in Minerva's Tower.

PHILOSOPHIC month—forty days.
Milk curdles, occult libraries open.
Palace shudders. Corpses dangle from Nuremberg Gate.
Falcon of pride aloft. Creation
ordered under Aries.

MOBS uttering plaintive cries
surround Viceroy. Quickening vapor.
Chamberlain stabbed. Regicide prepares.
Barons gamble quadrant to quadrant.
Ambassador flees Vienna.

FALLEN angels conceal cleft hooves.
Conspiracy born of conjecture. Blackness
depurates. Theurgic Stone.
Ayuperes.

WOLF devouring dog.
Imperial Guard!

TYRANT defers to sentiment. Gazelle.
Dromedary. Scribe. Silhouette. Starling.
Say promises are violated, chaos encouraged—
what should engender the Magnum Opus?

PLANETS cling to their grooves, sectarian times depart.
Fish-wives and merchants lift wondering eyes.
Weasel. Shrew. Vulture explores liver.
Fire. Hail. The best suborned.
Azael. Azazel. Samael.
Mahazael.

TIMIDITY begs the hour.
Birds dip and flutter, shrieks
from the dungeon. Shrieks from the cock-loft.
Does blazing Sol at his zenith distract the wind?
Does he resurrect the fallen cedar?

THIRD ballot. Osprey.
Juventus.

JEWS speak of safety among liberal Turks
where Sulemain forbids persecution.

THINGS of themselves dissolve. Equinox condemned,
moving tongue cut out, living body burnt.
If we appoint Jehovah our witness

do we ratify misconduct?
Behold the generous servant of God
dispense absolution against victorious enormity,
extremities bloodier than a barber-chair.
Let the King number his grapes.
Valefar! Pruslas!

Granaries bulge. Famine regenerates. Protestant
legion, anger foretold. Populace betrayed.
Lances cross, matter festers.
Subsidies mount,
frogs rain from clouds,
ideas too late relinquished.
Say this was a chance occurrence,
to claim otherwise would argue disorder
more onerous than indifference. Disgrace and
iniquity stride toward us—striding with long strides.
Chancellors stirring entrails of an ox
register gross displacement.

Azure light expands,
half-globes pried apart.
Morenius the Adept
sickens,
dies.

Bathim!
Loray! Johavam!

TIMES prove full and cloudy,
assertions startling,
promises improbable and huge.

SATURN ascendant,
conflict among elements,
growth of precious catholicon.
Miraculous Infant swaddled in white
conceived with the fourth quarter of one grain
upon eight ounces of Quick-silver. And it spoke our future
with a loud voice—Mercury standing out of flux,
congealed like yellow wax. Five soft grains!
But for a whirlwind that came boiling
jagged with thunder and rage
unification was ours.

MINISTERS fall. Atrophy.
Covenant. King belittled by Queen.
Duplicitous heir consumed.
Anubis. Cerastes.
Fifth vessel boils.

SILVER taste bespeaks treachery,
nothing lacks it. Deputies quarrel.
Jester stricken. Resident bodies
exude monkshood. Nightshade.
Banewort. Death camass.
Hellebore.

Upas.
Greyana. Fox-glove.
Androgyne. Ostrich. Wild Goose.

AUTUMN ripens along the hedgerow.
Aged Lion prances, gold in maceration.
Red sub-serves the second,
white is third. Interior ferment.
Chymistry gains without,
alchymistry within.

ONE door closes, another opens.
Gilded Peacock screams at dawn.

REGENT bends to his devotion. Sealed epistle
divulges the malevolent nature of man.
Metallic seeds rankle, putrefy,
spiral toward conjunction—progression
followed by retrogression. Gold simmers heavily.
Vermin flee a body that is damned,
courtiers disdain a riddle.

DOOMED Prince separated from castellan
mews and frets. Oxen do not love their butcher,
fishes the fisherman. Twelve ducats assuage foolish Guard.
If gold speaks, other tongues fall silent.
Roman slaves wear iron rings.
White Castle rots.

𝕬NIMUS of our deity casts forth his shadow.
Aliment changes to blood, truth born to adversity.
Long-winged hawk rises whistling
from its master's fist.
We walk a path without turning.

𝕷ETTER intercepted. Partridge!
Harbinger of catastrophe.

𝕱OURTH ballot.

𝕱ORÄU! Chorion! Gyascutus astride mephitic wind.
Crocodile dancing on air. Perseid
bound to the stake.

𝕵ESTER escapes!

𝕬NTI-CHRIST to arrive on horseback
disguised as a merchant dressed with scales,
dressed with a long fur coat. Or he comes prancing—
obsequiously bowing—senescent actor liquid in rhetoric
exclaiming and prophesying to serve himself
weak principalities.

𝕳ONOR fled from sacred places,
sellers and buyers infest the temple.
Arrogance prevails, transmutes.

$\mathcal{A}$MBASSADORS assert infallibility.
Imperator orders cookies baked to his likeness.
What draws the moving pendulum aside?

$\mathcal{A}$IR to water,
water to earth. Athanor
yields brimstone and orpiment
decocted from bowels of the unclean. Corruption
precipitates. Darkness reinstated.

$\mathcal{L}$UNA welcomes Aries, chymists labor. Metal albifies.
Blind Lamb seeks inspiration after his heart.
Serpent writhes in jaws of Leucrocuta—
twelfth key. Valentinus says no more.
Spirit vitrifies ninth vessel,
communion disturbed.

$\mathcal{L}$ET verities be subject to observation,
let one hand grasp the flame.
Does not the swift glance of a lynx
penetrate walls? Are not tides inextricably
buckled to the moon? Is not a mirror darkened
if it reflects a dishonest face?

$\mathcal{C}$LOCK chimes,
morning slants to the sea.
Clouds rush westward, vines withdraw,

elements converge. Yellow fire above, adverse
and darkling atoms. Mercurius born.
Currus triumphalis antimonii!

Sᴜʟᴘʜᴜʀ submits to gold. Deceit. Complicity.
Tyranny persists, misery coagulates.
Cockerel atop dung-heap beats his wings.
What insect crawls best? Jeptha—
that which bites the deadliest. Conscience
a pebble tumbling in currents.

Fɪᴠᴇ hanged. Rebis. Tincar.
Zaaph. Indrademic Stone. Comerisson.
Imperator like a snake warns of his coming.
Zahau prescribes deadly bolus.
Corno! Flute!

Mᴀɢɪsᴛᴇʀɪᴀʟ features anointed
with honey and milk. Bodies fall to earth
out of their appetite for rest.
Privileged lips taste soil.
For every subsultus
Probatum.

Vɪᴠɪꜰɪᴇᴅ with flame
the Son strides forth armed
as warrior. Dragon avoids light,
darts among crevices.

MAN of Copper gives. Quick-silver denies,
watery substance accepts. Things interweave to separate
afresh. Thunderclap. Wild Goose ensnared, struggles,
forces mingle to combine. What was moist
withers, blossoming late. Omens
distend at the altar.

BEWARE the sharpened feather of a bird,
beware the tongue's thin leaf.

YESTERDAY shakes upon its foundation.
Sheep with boneless legs conceived at Nuremberg.
In Krakow a chicken with two beaks. Sanguine crosses
emerge from clouds over Delft. White faces in hollow log.
Pelican resuscitated after death. Mistrust gathers,
nations rave. Time waits at the door.

JEHOVAH is equitable but fierce.
Adepts welcome initiates.
Euphrates. Baurach.
Favonius.

PLUMED helmet. Nightwatch.

BEARDED atheling embraces Monkey. Crone
depends upon her staff. Hog. Owl. Black Cape.
Hook and Sickle. Banewort. Eclegm. What is,
or was, devoured by Jackal. Novices
whisper, gesticulate.

Subordinates bow,
mutter agreement. Toarech.
Colchotar. Jester attends funeral train.

Apostate world drifts, gathering waste. Rook.
Knight. Bishop. Pawn. Presiding forces
advance. Gall and deprivation.
Horror and a mad noise.
Lucifuge! Rofocale!
Iehous!

Water trickles from rotted oak,
soldiers behead multitudes,
sects encouraged.
Dissension,
swirling discord.
Crows hop toward carcass,
sycophants applaud.
Gallows burn.

Conspirators disperse, tide
encroaching.

How should a despot know humanity
except he taste its blood?

Hooked beak of eagle signifies death,
glorious wings out-stretched
equal apotheosis.

Dawn. Church bells. Shrovetide.
Mouse turd. Cat skull. Leg of wild dog.
Kerotakis. Bellows. Tongs.
Crumbled parchment.
Blighted fruit.

Tempest afflicts macrocosm—rain-spout,
fire, lightning. Colic, spasm,
fever, ague and dropsy afflict microcosm.
Nux vomica the panpharmacon.
For imperial madness
no restorative.

Betis! Mother of Science stands forth.
Revelations unwanted, loathsome.

Philosophies, religions,
histories, poesies,
fables and art proceed from Saturn.
Prophecies in Fourth Monarchy,
summit of truth.

Savage events predict their course.
Blood of the oppressed stains church timbers
at York Cockerels flutter in the sky above Amsterdam
preceded by horrific explosions. Angels wield fiery axes
over Budapest. Albino ravens on streets of Geneva

attack carriages. Gibbering nuns of Saint Agnes
deliver mute hunchbacks. Fountain erupts at Leipzig,
rages beyond control. Nothing occurs by chance.

MERCURIC cloud above Polish castle.
Scythes break, lepers moan.
Spiders hurry across the wall.
Rats awake. Ships wallow, founder.
Cygnet dies. Masses unburied.
Comet trails glistening particles.
Meteor scarifies Andromeda.
Sheep discover the taste of men.

BLIND woman sees fire in valley.

ANTIMONY deployed without intervention
coagulates, dissolves, albifies,
proceeding out of yellow,
culminating in black.
Clasyabolas!
Abigar!

FLUID surges, froths toward the rim of a universe
where mirage begins. Hemispheres unite.
Three suns congregate. Antaeus.
Arch of Heaven convulsed. Alien matter.
Sulphur obscures fifth vessel,
reduction of two by six.

RAMPANT Lion enters
escorted by apprentices.
Scorpion. White ash.
Causes age. Disintegration.

THOSE that study kabbalistic books,
unearth cities buried in the sand, listen for midnight
at the wall, what answer do they bring?
What should the answer be?
Minotaur. Cockatrice.

WAX melts on flagstone hearth,
gold overflows cupel. Chrysopoeia triumphant!
Trinity transmuted—blistered sand,
emerald glass. Centaur gallops,
resurgent. Alembic sings of tomorrow
and tomorrow and tomorrow.

EXOLUTION. Extasis.
Liquefaction.
Palingenesis invisible, indivisible.

LIGHT the queen of colors.
Furies ascendant,
cunning spirits play across centuries.
Was the Magisterium to blame
or those that sought it among false principles?

THE needle of Das Narrenschiff
does not waver. Out of each the next.

NEITHER beginning nor end
has Ourobouros.

TRUMPET. Drums.
Pike. Halberd. Torches
advance. Knight wearing golden armor
hesitates, bloody gauntlet lifts golden visor.

Rumors of a wandering magus conceived in heresy and mistrust that would
resurrect us before the gates of Prague . . .

𝔚ᴇ ᴀʀᴇ told that Time is a brisk wind bringing forth each hour some fresh proportion, and as our thoughts hourly change and narrow and differ without respite and are kept secret from all, so it happens with Time. Yet who is able to calculate the wind's edge, fathom such mystery and purpose?

𝕿ʜᴇʀᴇ must be something within us surpassing reason, which goes by several names and is the cause or source of controversy, enabling us to discern spiritual truth. Yet we find shadows cast up from imagination which coalesce, and intersect, and divide so that we cannot rest but lie bewildered.

𝕬ʟʟ things have been provided, they grow and flourish unassisted. Hence each mineral may choose its shape as does each flower. But if a man expects to employ or benefit from natural goods he cannot be complacent. We acknowledge that Iron is

Iron, yet not by itself does it change into an axe or a knife or a ploughshare. Similarly, Corn would not choose the shape of bread without human guidance. Thus we assess each product.

From the perceptible being of a thing, its nature manifest through sensible properties, haply we recognize its intent. Yet high matters arch on Creation's order, so do they oppose confident exposition. Now whereas the purpose of vegetables, herbs, insects, animals and birds is not difficult to surmise through voice, texture, pigment or shape, humanity's direction resists exposure. Hubris intervenes.

That the corpus of Man be diversely mathematic, we admit, since when he stands upright with his arms outstretched and his heels together he makes an equilateral triangle, the mediety of which coincides with his genital organ. And if a circuit were to be inscribed from this point touching the apex of the skull with the arms positioned diagonally so that their fingertips meet the perimeter, and if the feet be separated by an interval equivalent to that which separates the head from the fingertips, such a circle might be divided into five equal parts. Now this we comprehend, being prepared to demonstrate, but of innumerable suppositions that we hear professed which bewilder and horrify us, we plead much ignorance. Man is the vas insigne electionis, he incorporates all. Therefore was he meant to be the stronghold of discovery and thus does he become the fittest subject for alchymic labor. He is the alembic supplied with precious material whose superiorities and inferiorities we would segregate. What is he if not a constellation suffused with strength to ignite the evening? Why has he been fenced with grace if not to rule the stars?

IT IS stated that Man was compounded out of astral dust since his intelligence refracts light from many sources that furnish him. Still, disparate assemblies reiterate how few have found God, seeing only a distant reflection that reflects some other. Recipes for glory and wealth conspire against him, misadventures and schemes coalesce to debauch his patrimony and make him an unstable thing amid the redolence of moving flesh so that he languishes, bewildered by musical notes, ceremonies and reputations, profit and loss, so that he persists in elementary views of what he thought promised. And all of these dispositions conjoin to agitate his spirit until he appears to be a mute addressing others ignorant of his language who seeks refuge in fearful pantomime—a charade of sighs and grimaces.

IF WE look upon Man as a little world, or Microcosm, being drawn from planets and stars and earth and other elements, we propose that he must be quintessential. But why? Because four integers constitute the materiate world, accordingly he must be fifth and tends upon what destiny was implanted by nature at his conception.

WE HEAR that as our God undertook to provide excellence and beauty and peace He perceived nothing more liberally endowed than Himself. Therefore, conceiving with His mind a substantive universe, He imagined it to be no different from

His own Self. Therefore, humanity occupies a sphere coexisting among a plethora of others which are identical in majesty, harmony and indivisibility.

Now, if we assume that we are shaped after God's image we cannot help but ask upon consequences. Were we found rational or irrational, and to what cause? Say we discard logic while genuflecting to assurance, what legacy waits? Which passage leads from a labyrinth of error? Citrinity fails to enlighten us nor how the wind stands in Greece, so we proceed intermediate between heaven and hell. Ours is futile dust made with ravening flesh and soft clothes, a perishable morsel. Thus we decline, recreants ignoring intellect, tumbling into earth's receptive lap.

We hear it claimed for Light that because we cannot exploit through number, measure or weight the tenuity of its elements, and because through chymistry we neither catalogue its form nor trap its essential spirit, Light describes a superiority to rival greatness. We offer this without angust metaphysic, we order no candle for inspection, arguing that the highest realm of ideas and archetypes is but a shadow, a semblance of beatific glory. Then how much more so is our immutable and faeculent world, the meager image of predominance.

Divers instances of transcendent things may be observed to succeed out of others while requiring the annexation of nothing extraneous, such as milk coagulated into whey or butter or cheese, or purple grapes becoming red wine, or the determined moth which contrives to manumit its body from the caterpillar. We watch each progression from form to form, each essay at completion through perceptible stages of imperfection.

CONTEMPLATE the galloping horse. Never does he change into a lion, although if a lion feasts on a horse the vanquished reappears bearing the likeness and silhouette of the victor. So is each substance ultimately capable of transfiguration. But while we restrict the hand to four necessary fingers, we ascribe to our succession multiple ways.

HAS not each herb been offered a profile corresponding to its essence? Certainly. And as these lineaments concur with what that herb is, so must the exterior physiognomy of each man approximate the condition of his interiority and make up a name more fundamental to him than his own, so that one might be called lark, goat, wolf or hedgehog. By stance and by carriage, upon timbre or balance of voice, by the resonance of laughter or from the passion of his stride—whether he walk with redoubled arrogance or timorous with doubt—we may assess his spirit as close as we scale the maturation of an elk by the size and complexity and thrust of its antlers, or as we deduce the private medicinalities of blossoms, nuts and legumes through odor, aspect or taste. Each discloses what he is. Who could label a fox a sheep? Who would take the hovering kestrel for a turtle dove? Each proceeds to his disposition like the creeping crocodile which cannot turn its head.

Now if a Prince elects to build a city he will construct moats and towers and passages and markets and citadels and fountains and everything else to agree with his design. Well, if a man is able to do this, think what marvels nature can accomplish. Is it not true that nature cripples one man, blinds the next, and makes another simple? Yes. But why? Because of a pattern to which he must contribute, hence no disproportion may ensue. So we understand how nature will create what she anticipates. What was destined for Blackness will be tinged by that color, thus with every hue and countenance, as the nettle's purpose is to sting, or what is intended to purge will be an equisetum, or that which polishes and smoothes will be made into a smiris. Things are given their signature that we know to what end each was devised.

It is clear how animate or inanimate things subsist with equal dignity, not one reigns supreme. Because our globe is transient and full of darkness must it be decried as inferior to the sun? No. Are sublunar unities less than those fixed in the firmament? Or what of the Spider? Was he not made equivalent to the Perch? Each entity controls an empire of its own.

Listen. What should the Son obtain from his Mother and Father to make him proud? How does he think himself more than they? Do not his qualities succeed from them? Look to his entirety. What is he save a grumbling stomach led by a grasping brain—troubled, helpless, naked underneath his first cloak—governed by the gnomon's journey which mocks his passage

across a dial. Yet we hear many complain how our God has fab-
ricked the world. Unlike phlegmatic animals, these will be
asked before a Throne to render accounts.

WELL, since our Lord comprehends all, humanity inherits
His indefectible complement of knowledge, and as nothing
might be found in humanity, nor any propension in which there
is not a small facet of divinity to be registered, so shall a man
complete himself by gazing upon himself. But at length every
man must look up toward that image whose likeness he is,
whose resemblance he should adore and whose superiority he
is expected to recapitulate, just as the lodestone consummates
itself among mineral.

NOW we hear that Saints will not carry out their existence because they disdain idolatry and because of the simulacra that
men carve, therefore they do not live adjacent to us. And we
contend that our thoughts must supersede our images, which
must be our highest ideal. And the higher that we rise to express
ourselves, so shall what we have chosen to think. And if we adhere to this we are not apt to be disappointed in spite of vicis-
situde, but if we would subsist without it then we will hurry off
by ourselves on some fatuous search which resembles dreaming. We know how Jacob went to sleep beside the Ladder, which
symbolizes divinity within reach. And we are appointed to wake
at a propitious hour.

WE HAVE been instructed by the author of Novum Organum
how cosmic structures shall remain inaccessible to apprehension through mortal sensibility, which provides as it does twelve

thousand ambiguous paths, similitudes, complex windings or deceptive regressions and knots of nature, while the credulous mind, being unable to distinguish truth from egregious perversion, does but misconstrue to compound and defraud our innocence.

Rabbi Ben Jochai asserts that the unequivocal presence of Man affirms the validity of all things apparent in heaven or upon earth, because nothing could exist before the human prototype. Matter subsists by us, within us. And this seems demonstrable, since without us who could imagine a world? Who should inhabit the uncircumscribed court of memory?

We are told that Man may be likened to an imperfect embryo which grows vulnerable to delusions of sense and phantasy until it has been rectified, neglecting every encumbrance. This we regard as the comprehending whole of alchymic law: to incite or seduce all men from disproportionate sensibles toward immanent coherence. Upon this philosophical premise and by this path we approach Heaven's Gate.

Suppose we give up our tenement, what is morality's foundation? From the cabbalistic book of Zohar we learn that when a soul undertakes to visit earth but fails to acquire the knowledge for which it descended, so that its signature is obliterated, it occupies a subordinate body until purified by repetitious and cognitive experience. Then this must be our fundament.

WE PRESUME the weightiest form to be that of earth——matrix of minerals which keeps secretly to itself while furnishing life to every dependent. So ring the highest bodies overhead where immaculate light collects and stars are roweled about, sending down virtue.

WELL, if we consider how we were bequeathed this universe we think its revolutions ought to be organized for our edification——spiral movements dispersed by that broad parabola of stars which nightly monitors our home and refuge. Now if Utopia be celestial, then Man's spirit should prove next to God. And therefore, if Man's wealth be laid apart in ephemeral or fading objects, we propose that the impoverished spirit must labor among lost and fading deities.

SINCE initially the universe was propounded by God, by Him it is meant to be concluded. Divers examples could we cite of mechanical shape or design drawn from unorthodox craft, yet how could a man benefit by exchanging spiritual belief for the joy of weighing aether, for the fugitive pleasure of calculating a pendulum's arc? What deposition has this? Should the years reverse their flight?

TO ALL things God offers an appropriate term of existence whether for mischief or good, and the fleshy life of a man compared to the duration of his Creator is miserably quick because God will persist after flames incinerate the world. Man does not last long, his term is narrow, and throughout fitful years he feels oppressed by voices riding the wind, assailed by something that pities lesser beings.

Anxious for culmination, Man arrives turned with many sides and listens for the spinning murmur of creation at the hush of the seventh day. Like the curve of a plate that is tossed on a wheel, or like cast-gold ornaments made in tropic lands, or like a pool of smelted iron, so was his future determined by Providence which takes care neither to shift nor cancel.

We propose that holiness was cast apart from the Church by God Himself, since to whom else should we attribute dignities, prebends, curacies, altars and rectorships being staked at dice, lost, won, or offered in exchange for mistresses, for gold? We see with what ease priories, abbeys, readerships and professorships may be purchased by the first wheelwright or chapman or peasant or thief to waggle his bulging purse underneath a bishop's nose. Does not surpassing conceit adumbrate the midnight hour? Have not men dishonored reason to perpetuate unspeakable absurdities? Yet do we depart from the animal—obtaining no dispensation from the issue of our thought.

Now the humblest creatures obediently conform to instinct because this tends to the preservation of their existence, which they perceive to be their total happiness and welfare. But it is different with men who feel disposed to preserve whatever is mortal about them, yet feel a higher obligation. And it is to this that they owe their allegiance. Therefore Man rightly has been named Microcosm, formed upon the image of a Creator, and the abrégé of His work. And the universe was completed with Man's formation because it was necessary that a universe be created in stupendous proportion before reducing it to hominal limits. Now as the cat inevitably is treacherous, the lion bold, the dog compliant, and the lamb gentle, so might we conjecture on the propensities of Man. But at this we are deceived since he is full of excess. And we hear prophecy of a dawn against which every contrivance fails. What do men do except light tapers, pray and copulate until the advent? Is not their reproduction the palmary act of dispassionate nature? What makes it a concern of mortals to become immortal and grasp at futures surmounting this? Philosophers that opine a scalding destruction of the world have not dreamt upon a reduction of mortalities into glass—which is vitrification.

CENTURIES testify to the existence of an Immaculate Teacher by whom all nativities are constituted, yet are we engaged with dubious adventure, blind, troubled by a whistling among the senses, our days mortgaged, arguing externals that yield new burdens and perplexities in proportion as they increase. So we ask upon history's course: might this be the register of fallacious dispute and mischance, of infamous sophistry? Does an instant arrive when fraud and perversion suffocate the soul? How should we exercise judgment against ourselves? Where is hermetic treasure manifest?

REFLECT how infirm faculties of the mind rally to desperate imposture, how the highest subserve the lowest, how deceit and hubris graduate from private into public circumstance, casting a furious heritage across civility. What engenders wisdom's root? Who shall take the measure of wisdom's leaf? Which among us has visited the antechamber of understanding?

Suppose the crypt of Christian Rosenkreutz should fly open, would reformation follow? And what of the Lord Poemander—where does He abide? What covenant approves our dissembling fall and transformation? Or the alchymist at his work-shop, how could he distil incomprehensible matter from its curse? Complexities, enigmas, all that is or is not—all provide their statement and we awaken disgruntled. Disappointments cloud the dawn. We search after the luxuries of intolerable flesh and transient comfort, swift things that cause grief. Ambiguous oracles stupefy us. We become fearful and twisted, persuading ourselves it is good to interpret or prophesy.

Zoroaster, counseled by angels, renounced Heaven's favorites that he might bequeath alchymic magistery through hieroglyphs, circumscribing the boundaries of rectitude. So did Heliodorus in Thessaly give up a bishopric at Triccia rather than accede to the verdict which condemned his meditations. And therefore we believe superiority must be that which rises out of critical intercourse. And we think Man was constituted from two bodies, one visible, one invisible, and we say the latter defines us.

We assert that conscience, being unable to err, cannot sin but acts in solitude, approving or disapproving, so it is incorruptible. Thus, if we remark of any man that his conscience was bad, we speak not of a faculty but of some subject, which conscience has disavowed. And should any man persist at what has been rejected it is plain that the unicity of his being will shatter because he has plucked sour fruit and was driven aside, exiled from Paradise, and the frame of his recovery will be in doubt. Consequently he wanders from desert to desert seeking readmission to the triangular garden where he was born, which he considered his own.

As surely as Jehovah charged miners with the onerous task of purifying ore so that mineral wealth may be extracted, so did He enjoin each alchymic physician to reconstitute Mankind. Once the body becomes reconciled with the spirit, delivered of gross impurity, Man will come striding forth to stun the universe with his eminence. Who could dispute his legacy were he to embrace the morning star?

The signature beneath which each hermetic novitiate labors we say is the Cross. This must be true because Man resembles an infant that was privileged to stand upright, surmounting what has determined him in order to observe and to approve his own validity. Therefore, Man makes himself subservient to that lacerating solitude which follows upon perception. Accordingly he feels anguish throughout his life, and dying takes precedence over complacent animals. Such is the Crown he was given, such is the Sceptre.

We ask what becomes of religious prophets in our impious age. We recall how twelve merchants from Genoa sailing past Tunis wondered at the radiance that issued from a pyramid of rock, so forthwith put ashore and discovered the bloody corpse of Raimundus Lullius, stoned by Mahometans for whom the message of Christ's apotheosis aroused unspeakable rage and loathing. That a man be right or wrong at his judgment seems no matter, he makes a beacon either way.

FROM the orbit of the firmament we watch lights cast out by an astonishing hand that has determined their course, the pace and circuit of each—which ascends or declines—because no single thing can be superior to its equivalent and each was meant to fulfill its indecipherable purpose. But as we inhabit a stationary earth oblivious to its end, with faint ideas of Genesis and listen to reverberations of faint voices, how could we not feel subject to limits, like the helpless Mussel twisting against umbilical sinew. We ask when the light of life, which is the Golden Fleece, shall diffuse its glory around the body of the seeker.

LET us not abbreviate the curricula of philosophy nor grind and quibble against our lot. Why suck and chew a withered globe of dreams? Rather, let us like Synesius feel gratitude that we have been endowed with two pairs of eyes, one above, one below. Let us not compare our stipend to that of the Sun, nor to pleasant exsufflations of rising planets, nor to those circuitous pathways of love and remembrance nor of moments which affront and persecute the day by ordering each gesture, none of which can we establish, since the wisest instructors of chymistry and theology and mathematics have proved unable to document their existence. False exits delude us. Thus we pause, undecided between painted openings.

THERE is concealment to Metaphysic, but for every science its key, earthly or unearthly, since otherwise we are lost and travel perplexed, aggrieved, solitary and disconsolate. The benefit of learning we equate with that of experience, troubled, passive yet querulous, inciting what we deplore while pursuing moderate charities, afraid and censorious, seeking disparate comfort beneath senseless tides of music, but like an empty barrel booming portentous sound.

ARE we not quick to observe the beauty of an uncurled rose? Yet superior attributes manifest themselves while the form disintegrates. And much as we annotate divinity with Galen's De Usu Partium which we consider equivalent to the philosophy of Suarez, so with a single flower do we forecast the intent and progress of universal renovation that makes up prismatic images of joy and to all changeable things their changeless inclination.

NOW there be many coarse movements to earth with equivocal shapes like Egyptian tricks, or that famous river Arethusa which loses its current one place only to rise up distant. Thus the world is as it was while men reiterate their lives round about the periphery, complete with flexible judgment. So must each anagogic philosopher seeking first principles theurgically prepare himself by passing among incandescent solutions and dissolutions and ordeals with corrosive tests. Indifferent to popularity will he advance from Centricities to Extremes, visiting the Indies—both greater and lesser—by which men implicate heaven and earth, Daphne or Phoebus, considering the harmony in liberation.

Now the chymist with his trade prepares to analyze and distil and refine occluded liquid, whereas an alchymist at his craft sets forth to direct the novice through qualified reflections, and therefore he must demonstrate how the Magnum Opus begins. At first the initiate will observe Nigredo, or retrogression, during which components are relegated to primary constituents. Next appears Rebirth, while shadows reorganize their elements. Third appears the stage of Albedo during which matter whitens. Last he observes Rubedo, symbol of finality when transcendent matter surpasses yellow—whereupon an Imperial Infant arises beneath whose aegis the bitterest dregs and sords of humanity shall be protected.

Let us say our novice invests the Stone with its huge reward. He would not privately hold this talent for his collection of dry appointments but commit everything to his brothers, meditating upon how he was provided a treasure among bones since he will be required to give accounts by an inflexible judge that abhors periphrastic words. And if he act properly according to his understanding, so in accordance with theirs shall others act. Now this is true, although we have neither touched, watched, nor listened to the atoms of divinity.

OPPOSED by two-fold labors of duality, because the secret of material transmutation promises neither more nor less than spiritual regeneration, the neophyte should undertake gnomic experiments against a foundation of inconceivable anguish, lest the crucible be shattered, lest he may vaunt irrational power. Nature we liken to a Sieve through which enlightenment may be assigned or withheld.

LET the apprentice know that what he writes or professes is not his own since all things precede and outlast him so that he has but one contribution, which is the pattern of their embellishment. Therefore he is but a transitory instrument to calculate uncommon shapes for common truth. Who would impeach the light?

FIVE centuries before Abraham marched down to Egypt, which was before the Deluge, Adam's grandson Hermes Trismegistus lifted the sacred chalice to his lips. Homage to this master, thrice-greatest, resting in his private apartment in Cheops' pyramid, from whose hand Alexander took the Tabula Smaragdina with that unmentionable formula. But to the covetous or delinquent graduate we would award false profit—a wealth of drifting ash.

LET it be understood how the temple of Solomon was erected with the help of Hiram and Queen Sheba. So shall the stone of the wise be perfected through successive circulations. Now this immaculate stone becomes the rock of Christianity, a Numinous Child whose essence is two-fold, whose exoteric nature grows manifest while the esoteric remains concealed. And we wonder if glass might not be compared to that stone like those fools among men who take up attitudes or aspects of color with all sorts of divers and contradictory shapes and without melting can be repaired, but stream from sight like pretty liquors poured on sand in whose soul the agent of transfiguration which we call holy grace has yet to act.

WE HAVE heard the voices of Commerce naming us possessed that conjoin poverty with dungbeds and urge metal upward, crushing egg-shell by the cast of sooty lamps to grapple at mystery, summoning old correctives to meliorate brutish residue, so much in exchange for a glimpse of incandescent yellow slag. Peasants quarrel, lie bugger, drink and shout upon scullery maids by the hedgerow while great discoveries flutter from patched bellows to pockets vacant as a skull. Such are the wages of hermetic philosophy. But let it be. We ask no unprecedented honorarium since by alchymic craft we transmute men to makers of prodigious dreams.

WE LEARN how Beguinius discourses with his Tyrocinium on the extraction of quick-silver from diurnal atmosphere, of oleaginous sulphur that is a viscid balm conserving the interior warmth of human organs as well as of alchymy's third hypostatic principle, or Salt, which resembles earth dryly encrusted, conferring brackishness and solidity with taste, thereby preserving all from putrefaction—counsel at once sacred and profane. And because we think it unwise to formulate answers prematurely, we repudiate disclosure through subscription to riddle.

We ASSERT that Solomon himself withheld the incomprehensible while thrice-famous Hermes earlier had sought an exaltation of imperfect metals through the development of quick-silver, which emulates gold in quality and weight but was prohibited from enjoying prosperity by crudities beneath the soil. Thus we expect Mankind to lament its future not unlike this metal denied a legitimate place on earth, or like a hapless beast watching Death examine the horizon. So we say of each object that it must be the fruit of its element and that its origin is revealed by the element to which it returns. Quick-silver regresses to poverty, nymphs to liquid, witches to the wind. Man himself protests, roils, and having poured out his gifts lies down wretchedly next to darkness. None can dispute this. Who would doubt that particular numbers possess secret magic? Who doubts that Apollo's music reverberated from the walls of Troy?

We ASSERT that the Red Lion, Tinctura Physicorum, beloved of five hundred authors but thought impossible to achieve, has been accomplished by Hali, Albertus Magnus and Hermes Trismegistus. We regard its nature as wholly indescribable since each distillation requires the presence of two adepts laboring in unimaginable harmony. Revelation of this formula would cause the sophist to grow blasphemous just as the venal might shiver with anticipatory delight. Therefore a claimant expects less than nothing, pointing to the Ladder of Paradise whose seven rungs correspond to seven vowels or seven planets, each comprised of a different essence. So this is an alphabet conceived in secrecy to withhold magisteric art from chapmen instructed at birth like rapacious hornets to pillage flowers, from commonalities trudging between Jupiter and Pluto.

WE BELIEVE vessels holding flatulent or vaporous palliatives should be ordered like the alembic because delicate spirits must be drawn through a slender neck. Consider the Giraffe which is famous for his generosity, unlike the Hippopotamus or the Bear, or barnyard Swine. Nature devises various forms and proposes for each creature that shape thought congenial to its animus. Nor can any one be what it is not. The Tiger—could he play a flute?

IS IT not imperative to mark a disposition among entities of individuality or of kind? Consider the wrathful Leopard who rushes and springs after his prey with little regard, which is extravagant. So does the insistent Harlot make bold and we call her mendacious. Also, there is a natural enmity and amity among beings which will command them to disperse or to rejoice, like the amiable Dog jumping and frolicking about the foot of its master while the cowardly Sheep rushes bleating from the Wolf. And so, being engrafted by nature, essences do not change, albeit we have seen herbs withdraw from their purpose to resuscitate the ailing and morient, stars deviate from their course to signal imminent events, and upon its passionate flight we have witnessed the Soul accomplish more than alchymic ligatures.

Wᴇ ʙᴇʟɪᴇᴠᴇ three elements unite in the Soul. The nutritive we share with vegetables, and with animals the susceptive, but rationality is our private possession. How excellently is Man arranged, how much more attractive than subordinate creatures, since upon his countenance drifting expressions indicate divine comprehension while his generative members display their exquisite and noble symmetry. So we dispute those Manichees who claim we were denied a throne on earth and announce them wrong in the argument. With its cornucopia of jewels and fruits this world was meant for our pleasure. But of various gifts bestowed upon humanity we would assert the greatest to be that of Philosophers who guide and escort and direct us through blazing thickets.

Nᴏᴡ are there not four elements to the square? Or the circle, where does it lead if not upward? Or the habitat of divinity, is not this triangular? Yet how do we compute the mathematics of Heaven? If it has neither beginning nor end its boundaries cannot be estimated and its embodiment we fail to construe.

Lᴇᴛ us say we admit sentience to the most frivolous weed, then what should be dismissed—left alone next to the gate with its face turned aside? What fails to share the mercy and beneplacit of our Lord?

$\mathcal{S}$UPPOSE that a man refuses to identify the evil he observes, how might he profit? Upon what watch was he ordered, if not to adjudicate? Do we define ourselves with consonant pieties, knitting the scattered remnants of what once was?

$\mathcal{B}$EHOLD the ancient fabric of our tapestry—how it deteriorates. Women have brought forth sightless basilisks dressed in scales, furious in hair and talons. Lord, with what unseemly confidence has Mankind usurped Thy vast prerogative. And do they call Thee Ourobouros?

$\mathcal{S}$o! WHO appears cloaked with rage? On this restful Sabbath what journey seems imperative? Saint Augustine has affirmed the existence of but one sovereign philosophy that was absent from the world since Time began, which is called Christian and has endured by passing through innumerable vicissitudes with many shapes of transgression and of wickedness, being rephrased and magically elucidated when Mankind is debased. And with its one office it has but one catholic watchword: Ye shall be born again.

𝕽umors of a wandering magus conceived in heresy and mistrust that would resurrect us before the gates of 𝔓rague have shut.